HEART TROUBLE

HEARTS AND HEALTH: BOOK 1

DJ JAMISON

ACKNOWLEDGMENTS

Writing "Heart Trouble" was unlike any of my previous endeavors because of the loyal readers who kept me engaged and motivated while drafting it. I have to thank everyone in my Facebook group DJ and Company for humoring me and cheering me on day by day.

Many thanks to my beta readers for their feedback, proofing efforts and appreciation of my work. Lydia, Susan and Otterpus, your input was helpful as always. A special thank you must go out to Cee Brown, as well, who provided nurse-proofing for my first foray into the medical field in my fictional world of Ashe, Kansas. I believe Ben is a better nurse because of her insights.

1

Ben hustled into the emergency room, his cheeks rosy and his brown hair tossed about by the wind.

It was a touch too long, and the brisk spring breeze had wreaked havoc on it as he drove into work with the window down, mainly because the window was no longer *there*. But at least the weather was mild. Thinking of what might have happened if vandals had broken out his window just a month ago was almost enough to make him shiver.

He was late to work, not only because he'd had to clean up glass from the street — there were kids in the neighborhood, for goodness' sake — but because a stray cat had decided to take up residence in his front seat sometime after the vandals struck.

Ben was a sucker for cute and furry — man or animal — so he'd rescued the poor tattered thing, though he was pretty sure the feline considered it abduction, as he did not go along willingly. The chunk missing from the tomcat's ear and the scabby lump Ben felt under one leg indicated he was a bruiser of a fur ball. Also, there were the scratches he'd drawn all along Ben's tender forearm.

Those still smarted. Good thing Bruiser was adorable

despite his lumps and bumps, with a black-and-white coloring that made his face look lopsided like he was some kind of feline court jester.

Jester. Hmm, that would make a good name. Ben rubbed at a scratch already scabbing on his flesh. *No, Bruiser was more fitting.*

"Ben, there you are!" the charge nurse said.

She didn't sound too irritated he was late, but there was something about her tone that caught his attention.

"Sorry, I'm late," he said, reaching out to grab the charts Alex had ready for him. "I'll shorten my break."

"No problem, hon."

Ben tugged at the charts, faltering when Alex held tight. He raised his eyebrows.

She leaned forward over the desk conspiratorially. He glanced around, noticing Dawn watching their exchange with amusement. Leaning in, he whispered theatrically: "What? Do I have spinach in my teeth again?"

Alex smirked. "No, but I thought you should know we have your boyfriend in Exam 3. I saved him for you, but you're late and he's in pain, so—"

The rest of what she said was lost under Ben's groan of frustration. "Seriously? When are you going to forget that story?"

She laughed lightly. "Never."

Ben tugged the charts, and she let them go. He took a step in the direction of Exam 3, before whirling back.

"It's not ... *him*, is it?"

He didn't need to say a name. Alex knew who he meant. Her eyes softened with sympathy. "No, hon. Just another—"

"Reckless biker," Ben interrupted. "Okay, I got it."

He turned on his heel and fast-walked toward the exam room, his cheeks still burning. Why did he always have to ask? Of course, Alex wouldn't have teased him like that if Tripp were in the ER.

He thought back to the day Tripp dropped him cold. They'd met up for a late lunch and a few beers, and he'd figured they'd go back to his place afterward as usual. Tripp wasn't the cuddly type, and while Ben was wishing for more — freaking beating his head against the wall trying to figure out how to push for more — Tripp met someone else. Someone who was somehow worthy.

Must have been some guy.

Ben had tried to hide his hurt, but Tripp saw it.

He'd told Ben he'd probably meet a doctor to sweep him off his feet. When Ben scoffed, saying doctors were assholes and he'd take a biker any day, Tripp had joked that Ben would meet the love of his life, injured in the ER.

Now, every time they had a biker in the ER, Alex made sure Ben got the chart and a few teasing remarks to go with it.

The love of his life a biker? Not damn likely.

He'd been an idiot about Tripp, but he'd learned his lesson. He wasn't cut out for winning the heart of a man who craved excitement.

He was a nurse. He spent his days changing catheters (he still wasn't used to *that* scent), jabbing needles into people (*very well, thank you very much*), and administering enemas (the shit had literally hit the fan on his first attempt; it was a wonder he'd ever wanted anal sex again).

He ended his shifts, more often than he'd like to admit, covered in vomit, blood or other substances that should remain unnamed.

Nothing about that was sexy.

But the man in Exam 3 ... he was sexy.

Ben drew the curtain aside in a rattle of sliding hooks, only to stop short. His breath caught in his chest.

The man before him was long and lean, so tall his feet hung

off the end of the bed. His light blond hair was a tousled mess against the pillow.

He was scruffy, pale fuzz barely darkening his jaw but roughing up what might otherwise be a baby face. Just now that jaw was clenched in pain.

The man turned his head at the sound of the curtain being drawn open, and Ben hurried to school his expression to the sympathetic friendliness he showed all his patients.

"Hey there," Ben said, stepping inside and tugging the curtain closed behind him. Casting a quick glance at his chart, he sought out his name. "Gage. How you feeling?"

He glanced up to see light blue eyes fixed on him.

"Been better," Gage said, his voice coming out hoarse. He gestured to his sheet-covered leg. "Got a little torn up."

Ben scanned the chart, gleaning the few details he could. It was a case of second-degree road rash caused by a motorcycle accident, along with a couple of gashes that would need sutures.

Geez, I hope Alex didn't have him waiting long on my account.

He was a little surprised to see the patient wearing a leather jacket over his hospital gown. The left sleeve was torn to shit, indicating he'd nearly scraped up his arm, as well.

"Interesting attire," Ben teased, as hooked the chart on the foot of the bed and made his way closer to take in the damage.

Lifting the sheet, he saw that Alex hadn't really left Gage to suffer untended while Ben rescued a stray cat. His leg had been cleaned and bandaged. Judging by the amount of bandages, covering a large stretch of calf and outer thigh, the man was probably hurting.

"Sorry," Gage said gruffly. "It was a little cold in here, and I hate hospital gowns."

"It is a bit like a refrigerator, isn't it?" Ben said with a smile. "I'm Ben, by the way. I'll be your nurse tonight. I'm going to just take a peek under these bandages and go browbeat a doctor into getting in here to take care of you. You haven't received anything for the pain, is that right? I'll try to get a rush put on that."

"That's okay. I told the other nurse I wouldn't need anything."

Ben lifted an eyebrow. That usually meant one of two things.

"So, are you an idiot with too much pride or a recovering addict?"

Gage stiffened, and his smile looked forced. "You don't hold your punches, do you?"

Ben patted his arm. "I'm a nurse, sweetie. We never do."

Gage's eyes widened at Ben's term of endearment. It didn't mean anything — except maybe that he was showing his gay — because Ben talked that way to all his patients. But Gage wouldn't know that.

Without waiting for the silence to become awkward, he stepped away to wash his hands in the small sink against the wall, then returned to the bedside.

"Just taking a quick look," he murmured, waiting for Gage's nod of approval before unfastening one corner of his bandage enough to get a look at the damaged flesh beneath.

He grimaced at what he saw.

The man had done a real number on himself. Angry scrapes covered his leg, and he was going to need sutures in two places. But everything looked clean and disinfected, so he reattached the bandage and slid the sheet up.

A smile tugged at his lips when, in the process, he glimpsed tight orange briefs under Gage's hospital gown. *Interesting underwear choice. This guy has a bit of flair.*

Glancing up at that battered jacket, he frowned. "Is the leg your only damage?"

Gage chuckled, and Ben's eyes shot up to his face. His lips smirked as he replied. "That's debatable. What kind of damage are we talking: mental, emotional or physical?"

Ben laughed. "I only deal with the physical, honey."

Gage's smile widened, and Ben realized how that sounded. He hurried to get the conversation back on track. Flirting with patients was not ordinarily something he did, and he especially didn't need to flirt with a biker. Despite what he'd said to Tripp, he was in no hurry to be another guy's fuck buddy until he got bored.

"What I meant was, that jacket is looking abused. Do you have any other injuries?"

Even as he asked, Ben grabbed the chart to skim over the details once more. Not that he didn't trust the patient, but he wanted to be sure he knew what had been detailed thus far.

"Jacket saved me," Gage mumbled. "I might have a few bruises."

Ben tsked. In addition to sutures, Gage was going to need a round of examinations to ensure there were no breaks or internal injuries to his body.

"Want me to take it off?"

Ben startled, glancing up. "What?"

"The jacket?" Gage said. "Do you need to see the rest of me?"

Ben bit down on his lip hard as images spilled through his mind. Even in a hospital gown covered by a leather jacket, Gage was a good looking man. His chest was firm and his shoulders broad. It was tempting to agree, just to *look* a little, after the dry spell Ben had experienced since Tripp dumped him.

That would be playing with fire, and he knew it.

Ben shook his head and replaced the chart.

"The doctor will make a more complete examination," he said. "Let me go hunt down Dr. Johnston. I'll scold him until he makes you his top priority."

Ben smiled his polite nurse smile and turned for the door. He needed to get out of that room before he drooled all over his patient.

Holy shit, he was a fucking idiot.

For the thousandth time, Gage asked himself why the hell he'd thought it would be a good idea to go out with a group of bikers for a guest column he was writing as part of the alternative journalism class he taught at the junior college.

He'd made a fool of himself in front of some Harley riders the Ashe Sentinel staff had convinced to help him. Apparently one of their former press guys had ridden with the group, and they were open to him experiencing a day in the life of a small-town biker. His column focused on jumping into new experiences in the community, and he'd sort of tuned out during the brief set of lessons they'd tried to give him.

Riding a bike wasn't difficult. Tons of men did it. Hell, teenagers did it. Yet, he'd somehow managed to get startled by a fucking squirrel of all things, swerve, lay the bike down and slide down the street.

To top it off, the bikers had laughed their asses off and taken pictures with their phones, generously offering to tag him on Facebook so he could use them with his column. *Assholes.*

Thankfully, one of them had called a friend to give him a ride to the hospital so he didn't have to come in by ambulance. *Talk about embarrassing.* Although that would have made for an entirely different column: "My first ambulance ride, by Gage Evans."

All in all, a seriously shitty day.

That combined with his aversion to any kind of drug use – prescribed or not – and he was in some pain. His leg throbbed rhythmically, and he was hyperaware of the blood traveling through his body, as it seemed his pulse wanted to beat right *there* under his injuries. Meanwhile, fire licked up and down the surface of his skin.

It was driving him *crazy*.

Then Nurse Hotness walked in.

The first nurse had been a nice maternal type, but this one was just shy of six feet with wavy brown hair and eyes to match. His skin tone was warm, nearly tan, and Gage would lay money he looked that way year-round, rain or shine. *Lucky bastard.* He wouldn't mind getting a look under those ridiculous scrubs, either. He hadn't thought it could be done, but Nurse Hotness made the drab, shapeless outfit look good.

He was warm and friendly, flirty even, and Gage had been pleasantly distracted until he left.

So, he was relieved when Nurse Hotness returned with a fairly attractive, if older, doctor trailing him. He was less happy to see the way the doctor's eyes fixed on Nurse Hotness' ass.

Looks like I can kiss my fantasies of a sponge bath good-bye.

"Good news, Gage," the nurse said, his lips lifting in a wide smile. "Dr. Johnston is here to properly treat you. So, I'll just get these bandages off and let him get down to the business of stitching you up."

"Thanks," Gage said, relieved despite the small spark of irritation that Dr. Johnston had more interest in watching Nurse Hotness than looking over his chart.

The nurse pulled over a rolling table, and set out a few supplies. Scissors, a small basin of water and antibacterial soap. He snapped a pair of gloves over what looked to be strong, nimble hands and picked up the scissors.

Gage looked away as soon as those hands reached his thigh. He didn't want to watch. The idea of his torn flesh made his stomach turn. He didn't much care to watch the doctor, either, who stood close behind the nurse. *Too close.*

Instead, he fixed his gaze on Nurse Hotness' face while the man's attention was otherwise engaged. His lids were lowered as he looked down to focus on his work, and Gage's eyes were drawn to his long lashes. They were dark like his hair, but there were a few lighter lashes mixed in, giving a few glimmers of gold.

Gage's gaze dropped to his mouth. The nurse's lips pursed in concentration as he worked, but they looked full and firm. Juicy even.

Jesus, stop objectifying the nurse. He's trying to do his job.

Just as he started to worry he might pop wood, a tug at his skin made him gasp and wince. All possibility of erection vanished.

Nurse Hotness looked up, regret in his big brown eyes. "Sorry, sweetie. But you're all ready for the doctor now."

He patted Gage's ankle, safely removed from the damage zone, and stepped back. When he did, he bumped into Dr. Johnston behind him.

"Oh, sorry," the nurse said, edging away from the contact. Yeah, he didn't like Dr. Johnston. Not like that.

Gage smiled, feeling his spirits rise, as the nurse made his way toward the door without a second glance at the doctor.

"Wait!" he called, and Nurse Hotness turned.

"What is it, hon?"

"Your name," he said, his voice going gravelly again with nerves. "What was it?"

The nurse smiled wide, warmth emanating from him in waves. "My name's Ben. Good luck, Gage. Maybe I'll see you around sometime."

"Okay, may— ow, motherfuck!"

The doctor chose that moment to slide a needle into him, and the asshole was not gentle. When Gage caught his breath enough to look to the doorway, Ben was gone.

It was a relatively quiet night in the ER, and Ben took the opportunity to catch up on paperwork at the admissions desk. With eyes locked on the glowing computer screen, he didn't see Alex approach until a snicker sounded in front of him.

He glanced up, took in her smug expression, and returned his gaze determinedly to the screen. His lips tightened in irritation. Her teasing was all in good fun, but he didn't relish the reminder of Tripp's rejection.

"Was he everything you thought he'd be?"

Ben tapped the enter key, submitting his update to the file on screen, then closed the window. Stepping back, he crossed his arms over his chest.

"Yep, Dr. Johnston was entirely what I expected."

Alex snorted. "You mean he stared at your ass and drooled. That *is* predictable."

Ben's cheeks went hot. "He did *not*."

Alex waved a hand. "Whatever, we're not talking about him. You don't believe me when I tell you, and that's fine, because I might barf a little if you got with him. I was asking about the hottie biker in Exam 3. Is there a new boyfriend in the cards?"

Ben rolled his eyes, silently searching for patience.

"You have a boyfriend?"

Ben startled, eyes refocusing to see Dr. Johnston had approached the nurses station and was watching him with a bit too much interest. *Hell, was Alex right?*

He cocked his head, studying the doctor's face. His skin was clear and smooth, and his features even. His eyes were placed a bit too close together behind his glasses, maybe, but overall, he was an attractive man. He looked more academic, perhaps, than Ben's usual type. He didn't have much in common with men like Tripp, who oozed macho appeal and were just a bit rough around the edges.

Of course, Ben could do with a man who was less like the ones who tossed him away without a second thought.

Ben couldn't hold onto a man's interest based on physical desire alone. He was cute enough to pick someone up for a one-nighter or casual dating, but not for the long haul. So, maybe he needed a man looking for something a little different.

His gaze strayed to the doctor's left hand, resting against the counter. A silver band rested on his ring finger.

Deal breaker.

"Yes," Alex answered for him when he paused too long. "Ben's got a boyfriend, and you've got a wife. And I've got my cat. We're all so lucky."

"Ah, yes, well." Dr. Johnston cleared his throat awkwardly. "I'd better get on with it."

He waved toward the hallway behind him vaguely and hurried away.

"Oh hey, that reminds me," Ben said, changing the subject before Alex could give him shit. "I have a cat, too, now!"

"Ooh, tell me everything. How did you meet? Is he handsome?"

"Holy crap, you did a number on yourself."

Gage jerked from the half-doze he was in, flinching with pain when he tried to sit up too quickly.

Chloe stood in the doorway, staring at his leg with an expression of fascination. He glanced down, relieved that the new bandages remained clean and dry, not a drop of blood in sight.

He'd tossed off the sheet shortly after the doctor gave him his after-care instructions because it was irritating the bandages. His hospital gown had ridden up in his sleep, exposing his bright orange briefs.

Christ, that was embarrassing. He hadn't given it a thought earlier; he'd been in too much pain. Had Nurse Hotness noticed his flamboyant underwear?

After the doctor stitched him up, he'd had to give up the small dignity of wearing his jacket over the atrocious hospital gown. The doctor had insisted on examining the rest of Gage's body. Apparently internal injuries were a concern if the bruising was too severe. He'd have preferred Nurse Hotness be the one to poke and prod at him, but he'd put up with it and the round of X-rays he was pretty sure he – and his bank account – didn't need.

He flipped the sheet over his crotch now that Chloe was in the room.

"Here, I brought you shorts, as instructed," she said, plopping a gym bag onto the bed by his hip. "Sorry I took so long. Play rehearsals took forever tonight. No one could remember a fucking line."

He scrubbed a hand over his face in an attempt to shake off his grogginess. He'd let the doctor prescribe a pain medication after all, because he was a fucking wuss and his leg hurt like a bitch. It was just extra-strength Tylenol, nothing narcotic, but as the pain faded, he'd crashed.

"It's okay," he said, unzipping the bag and pulling out a pair of basketball shorts. He didn't think he could handle pulling on a pair of jeans, or even sweatpants. "Can you grab my shirt from the pile over there?"

Chloe crossed to the chair where Gage's clothes were folded neatly. One of the nurses must have done that, because he'd tossed them in a heap on the floor when he'd changed into the hospital gown.

She shifted the pile until she found his long-sleeved T-shirt. He'd told them to throw away his ruined jeans, which were shredded to hell and stained with blood. But Chloe held up his leather jacket, examining the shredded outer layer on the left side.

"Jesus, Gage," she said, shaking her head, before returning to his bedside with the shirt. "Maybe you're not cut out to be a badass."

He ignored her comment, though he couldn't deny she had a point. He had zero desire to get back on a motorcycle. If that's what it took to be a badass, then no thank you. He'd just be a boring college instructor, but a college instructor who was still in one piece. He could live with that.

He started to lift the sheet, then paused. When he looked up, Chloe smirked at him.

"I already saw the tighty orangy's."

"You're hilarious," he deadpanned. "Turn around please."

She spun. "Oh my God, you're such a blushing maiden."

He chuckled as he flipped back the sheet and began easing the shorts on, first over his good leg and then ever so carefully up his damaged one. Chloe had gone to bars with him often enough, gay bars included, to know he was *not* shy.

"I don't need your lecherous gaze on me when I'm injured and vulnerable."

Chloe cackled, and a flash of pain hit Gage as he stupidly bent his leg.

"Fuck, fucking fuck! Stupid fucking column. Stupid idea. Stupid class!"

She turned around. "It was your idea, and you love teaching that class."

"Whatever," he muttered, modesty forgotten as he struggled to get dressed without causing himself even more pain.

She took pity on him and helped ease the shorts over his leg.

"Lift," she instructed, and he lifted his hips so she could pull them up over his ass. "There we go. Good boy."

"Fuck off."

"Is that anyway to treat someone you love?"

"Knock-knock!" a warm voice called, familiar enough to send a flutter through Gage's stomach. *Nurse Hotness!*

Ben pushed in a wheelchair. "Your getaway wheels have arrived," he said with a wink.

Damn, he was cute.

Chloe grinned as she looked from Gage – who had possibly perked up like a happy Cocker Spaniel when he heard Ben's voice – to the nurse entering the room. Warning bells went off in Gage's head at the expression on her face.

He tried to catch her eye, but she was busy giving his nurse a thorough once-over. Damn, he hoped he wasn't wrong about Ben being into men. He'd hate to have to kill his best friend.

"So, who are you?" she asked.

"He's my nurse," Gage said gruffly, giving her the stink eye.

"Oh, I see," she said, sounding a little too knowing, and considering how well Chloe knew Gage, she probably had already figured out his attraction to Ben. "Does your nurse have a name?"

Ben stepped forward, extending a hand. "Ben Griggs. Nice to meet you."

"Well, Ben Griggs, you do scrub up nice." She cast a look in Gage's direction. "Maybe that's why Gage hasn't introduced me? I'm Chloe, by the way."

Ben blushed. "Um, thanks. Nice to meet you, Chloe. I'll just leave this here if you want to push out your ..."

He left the statement hanging, as if waiting for someone to fill it in, and Gage hurried to comply.

"Friend," he said quickly. "Just a friend."

Chloe quirked a brow in his direction. "Right. This friend needs a smoke break." She glanced at Ben. "Do you mind pushing him out to the doors? It's been a long night."

"No problem," Ben said. His gaze moved to Gage. "I wanted

to talk to you about your after-care anyway. Unless she's going to be helping with that?"

Gage had already received instructions from the doctor, but he wasn't about to pass up an opportunity to talk with Ben a bit longer — and he definitely wasn't going to pass up the chance to make it clear Chloe was not his girlfriend.

"No," he said quickly. "We're not that close."

Chloe rolled her eyes. "Right. We're practically strangers. I'll be outside."

Ben watched her go, a look of confusion on his face. "Did I miss something?"

"Don't mind her. She's a drama teacher."

Gage swiveled sideways, cautiously lowering his feet to the ground. Grimacing, he stood, the stitches pulling uncomfortably as he straightened.

Ben pulled the wheelchair up close to the bed and locked it in place, then took hold of Gage's arm to help steady and turn him so he could ease down into the seat. Unfortunately, he was too focused on getting his ass in the chair to really appreciate the nurse's closeness.

"Thanks," he said, feeling exhausted once he was seated.

Ben unlocked the wheelchair and swung it in a circle, heading toward the hallway.

"So, it's important that you take care of yourself when you leave here," Ben said from behind him.

"The doc went over some instructions."

"Mmm-hmm, that's good," Ben said, but he was undeterred. "There's a danger of infection, you understand? You don't want to get gangrene."

Gang-what??!

Ben looked serious. "You know, turns green, oozes pus, leads to amputation?"

Gage shook his head, feeling a bit sick. Surely, his injuries weren't bad enough for all that.

Ben chuckled, giving away the joke before he could become seriously worried.

"Okay, that's just a little nursing humor. But you do want to keep it dry. Watch for the 3 W's: warmth, weeping and weather. I recommend checking every few hours."

"I think I get warmth and weeping, but weather?"

"Make sure the area surrounding your injury is not hot to the touch, is not oozing and doesn't change color. Come in immediately if you notice any of those things."

Gage nodded, still feeling a little disconcerted.

"You'll be fine, but I don't want to see you back here in pain. So, please make sure you follow those instructions carefully."

Gage tipped his head back, forehead brushing Ben's chest, his gaze locked on the strong line of his throat and underside of his jaw. The nurse was gorgeous, friendly and had a sense of humor (even if gangrene jokes were a bit out of his comfort zone). This was definitely a guy he wouldn't mind seeing again.

He blurted the words in his head without taking time to think them through.

"Believe me, the next time you see me in bed, it won't be painful at all."

The chair came to an abrupt stop, and Ben circled around to look down at Gage.

"Is that line supposed to impress me?"

Gage's eyes widened at Ben's irritated expression.

"I meant no disrespect," he said, his Southern roots coming out in force as he fumbled through an apology. "You're a great nurse, Ben. Today was awful and you made it more bearable, so thank you. I'm sorry if I offended you."

Ben smiled, though he looked uncomfortable. "It's okay. Just take care of yourself."

He returned to his place behind the wheelchair and pushed Gage to the exit. All the way there, Gage's heart raced, torn between keeping his mouth shut and manning up to ask Ben for a date. After that lame pick-up line, Gage was concerned Ben would immediately reject him, but nothing ventured, nothing gained, right?

Right, tell that to your left leg.

The doors whirred open, and Ben pushed him into a crisp evening wind. The smell of smoke drifted toward them from the right, and he glimpsed Chloe by the wall, a hand raised to pull the cigarette from her lips.

The thought that she'd arrive and Ben would go inside broke the hold on Gage's voice.

"Ben," he blurted, before the nurse could return to the building. "I, uh ... just— I ... shit. I wondered if maybe I could take you to dinner sometime?"

Ben stood behind him, making no move to circle around face-to-face. A long pause followed his words. Then: "I don't think that's a good idea."

"Because I said that stupid thing back there? I was just nervous," Gage said. "You're so gorgeous and talented—"

Ben laughed lightly, but there was a bitter edge to it. "Save the flattery, okay?"

Gage swallowed a lump of disappointment. "Okay. Just one question."

"Shoot."

"Why is it a bad idea?"

Ben shifted to the side, and he could finally see his face, though he couldn't discern his expression in the darkness.

"Because I don't date bikers."

"Oh, I'm not really a biker."

Ben's voice sounded skeptical. "Did you or did you not come in with road rash after laying down your bike in an accident?"

"Well, yeah, but—"

"You were riding a motorcycle, hence biker. I don't date bikers."

"But I'm not really a biker," he said again dumbly.

He heard the smile in Ben's voice. "Goodnight, Gage. Take care of yourself. No offense, but I hope I don't see you in here again."

2

Ben woke the next morning to sunshine on his face and the sound of a rip, followed by a loud yowl.

He lurched up, heart beating hard, to see Bruiser slide down the curtains like they were a carnival ride. He landed with a thump on the floor, ears laid back against his head in irritation. Claw tracks raked down one side of the drapes, which Bruiser's weight had pulled open enough to allow a direct beam of sunlight to hit Ben square in the face.

He squinted, still making sense of the scene in front of him, as Bruiser licked at a paw casually and then sauntered across the room. For a moment, Ben thought he might join him on the bed, but the cat slunk under the bed frame, back to his hidey hole.

Shoot. I should have grabbed him while he was out.

It was already 10 a.m. Not exactly late when you returned from work at 3 a.m., but Bruiser had an appointment with the vet at 11:30. Ben resigned himself to even more scratches when the time came to drag Bruiser out of there.

Rolling out of bed, he realized he was still wearing his scrubs. Glancing over his shoulder, he saw the neatly made – if wrinkled – covers. He'd passed out on top of the bed without changing. He had to stop doing that.

He wrinkled his nose as the scents of antiseptic, bleach and the underlying hint of blood wafted from him.

Ben briefly remembered dragging himself home, sharing some tuna with Bruiser, and heading to his bedroom with the intention of showering and changing for bed. He'd sat down on the bed while he listened to a voicemail from his mother – she wanted to talk to him about a health problem, she said, but then she always worried about her health – and at some point, he'd laid back and closed his eyes while her voice washed over him.

He spotted his cell phone lying beside his pillow. Rolling his eyes at himself, he grabbed it and plugged it in, then headed for the shower.

After cleaning up and dressing in jeans and a T-shirt, he headed for the kitchen to make breakfast and a bribe for Bruiser. He scarfed down his eggs, and scrounged up some more tuna to lure Bruiser out.

"Kitty, kitty," he called, while kneeling in front of his bed.

He spotted a tentative paw snake out toward the bowl, then pull back. He leaned down further, cajoling and pleading with Bruiser, before finally giving in to the sad fact he was going to have to pull him out.

He tentatively extended a hand under the bed when his phone rang, making him jump and snatch his hand back.

"Jesus!" he exclaimed, putting a hand over his racing chest and scrambling up to grab the phone.

"Hello?"

He was breathless after his heart nearly lurched right out of his chest.

"Ben?" He recognized his mother's tentative voice. "I didn't interrupt something, did I?"

"What? No," he said, laughing. God, did his mom think he was having sex? He should be so lucky.

The memory of Gage Evans surfaced. The way he'd stumbled over his words as he asked Ben out had been sweet, and his body had been pretty sweet, too. Ben wouldn't mind making a closer examination in different circumstances.

He's also another biker. Do you really want to go down that road?

Ben reluctantly pushed away the memory of Gage's sexy smile. He didn't need another emotionally distant man who was more interested in the initial adrenaline rush than a real connection, and yes, he was making generalizations, but they'd held true in his experience thus far.

"Honey, I have some bad news," his mom said.

Like a bucket of cold water, her words washed away any lingering thoughts of Gage or Ben's desire to have sex after six long weeks of abstinence.

"Oh, no. What's happened?"

"I think I have pancreatic cancer."

Ordinarily, words like that would terrify a loving son, and Ben loved his mom to pieces. They were close, always had been, and became even closer after his father died from a heart attack in his fifties.

That was also about the time Ben's mom became a hypochondriac.

Ben took a measured breath. It was important to hear her out, even though she was most likely paranoid. His father's death had devastated his mother and forced her to face her own mortality. She tended to fret over her health – turning the most minor complaints into fears of deadly diseases – and Ben being a nurse had only made that tendency worse.

They'd had several talks already about the fact Ben could not diagnose or recommend treatment for her ailments.

"Why do you think that?" he asked carefully.

"Well, I've been reading about the symptoms."

Ben bit back a groan. "Mom, you know you can't diagnose yourself. Whatever symptoms you read about could easily apply to another condition with the right set of circumstances—"

"I know, Ben, but I've been having so much pain," she said.

There was the ring of truth to her voice. She wasn't making it up. She never lied, but he could tell when she was stretching to make minor symptoms fit a disorder. Still, that didn't mean she had pancreatic cancer.

"What kind of pain? When did this start?"

"It's been off and on for months—"

"Months!"

"Well, at first I thought it was just a terrible stomach ache, but the pain was worse than I'd ever felt. Agonizing. But then it went away for a long time. I didn't want to worry you."

"Since when?" Ben said, losing his patience. "You're always talking to me about your health."

"And you don't like it."

Ben bit his lip, sufficiently chastised. "I'm sorry, Mom. I didn't mean to discourage you from talking to me if you're having pain. It's just that you theorize so much, and usually it's not ... I mean, it's just minor."

"So, do you think it's pancreatic cancer?"

"I really hope not."

Pancreatic cancer was fast and deadly. But abdominal pain could be caused by a lot of things: an ulcer, a bad gallbladder, indigestion. Or ... pancreatic cancer.

Only a doctor could diagnose her.

"I'll call the doctor and take you in for the first available appointment. This shouldn't wait."

If only to ease her mind, he thought. He was relatively certain it wouldn't be cancer, but you never did know.

"You're such a good boy. Thank you, honey."

"Don't ever feel you can't talk to me, even if I get cranky, Mom."

"Okay."

He hung up the phone and called the doctor's office to make an appointment with Dr. Alcott, explaining that his mother was having abdominal pain and he wanted her seen as soon as possible.

Fortunately, they had a cancellation and could get her in today. Unfortunately, the appointment was for 11:30, the same time as Bruiser's vet visit. He'd have to drop her off before taking Bruiser in for a set of shots that was not going to endear him to the cat even a little bit.

His scratched wrists stung just thinking about it.

———

"So, you actually crashed a motorcycle?"

Gage grimaced at the excited tone of one of the female students sitting in the front row of his class. Natasha sounded impressed, as if he'd crashed while attempting a daredevil jump instead of a leisurely Sunday drive.

Gage had returned to his classroom Monday morning more than a little embarrassed his first foray into "alternative journalism" had gone so badly. He'd designed a lesson plan that was part lecture, part practical application. As part of the class, he'd made a deal with The Ashe Sentinel to write guest columns that embodied the spirit of the likes of Hunter S Thompson and Tom Wolfe, if on a much smaller scale.

The idea was to become part of the story you were telling, and to provide the reader insights into new experiences that way, rather than as a third-party observer, as traditional journalism dictates.

It was a sometimes controversial form of journalism, but it

was generally accepted when done through column writing, features or magazine pieces — not to mention the ever more popular blogging in today's Internet age. Most newspapers wouldn't run that kind of narrative as news because of the obvious bias it required.

The students would do similar pieces for the college paper, but not until they were further into the class. Their projects would have to be approved by him, and he'd already checked motorcycle riding off the list. He didn't need a lawsuit on his hands if one of his students was as inept as he was.

"You don't look hurt. Did you make the whole thing up so the column would be more interesting?" Zane asked from a seat toward the back.

He was one of the more vocal students and obviously a skeptic. But this was a good transition into an actual lesson.

"Actually, good question. I want you all to listen closely," Gage said. "Alternative journalism is not fiction. There is always a basis in fact. What you're doing is living the story, not just writing it—"

"But don't some people say that Truman Capote and Hunter S Thompson made up some of the stuff they wrote?" Zane interrupted.

Smart kid.

It wasn't surprising Zane would know about Truman Capote, though they hadn't covered the writer yet. Capote had penned the novel "In Cold Blood" about a famous murder in Holcomb, Kansas. Anyone who grew up in the state had heard that story at one time or another. But the fact he knew of the academic debates about Capote's work indicated he'd done more reading on the topic than most of the students in the room.

Gage acknowledged the point. "There's been some debate over how literally to take their writing, yes. In the case of Hunter S Thompson, there were drugs involved, and who knows how that might have skewed the story, right? But at its heart, alternative journalism is still journalism. Can you embellish a little? Certainly. Can you paint more vibrant descriptions colored with your own perception? Yes. Should you change the setting or circumstances of events entirely? No. If you want creative writing, the English Department teaches those classes."

There was a twitter of laughter. The communications department and the English department were always a little at odds. The English instructors thought journalists were hacks who couldn't write a decent paragraph. On the other hand, most journalists were more concerned with telling their story than deconstructing a sentence.

Gage didn't doubt they were both a little unfair in their judgment of the other.

"So, what's your next topic?"

"Can we see your injury?"

"Go sky-diving!" Someone shouted.

"Ooh, Bungee jumping!"

Gage held up his hands for quiet. "Okay, okay. I'm glad you're all plotting my next great fall."

The students obliged him with a laugh.

"First off, no. You can't see my injury. It's under my clothes, and I'm pretty sure the college frowns on instructors doing a strip tease in class."

More laughter. Gage was in his element. He loved teaching, and he loved being the cool teacher. The funny one who made them want to come to class.

He continued.

"Mostly I hurt my pride, though, which is on display for you. Secondly, I'm still choosing my next topic. I'm on the fence between wall climbing at the center here in town and trying out horseback riding."

The students started shouting out their votes for what he

should do, and Gage let it go on for a moment or two before shutting them down.

"Okay, thanks. I'll think on it. Now, I want you guys to read Chapter 3 in your textbook. It'll cover some of the ground we talked about today."

There was the typical groaning and scraping of chairs as the students gathered their things and got up to leave.

Gage turned to gather his own belongings and head out. He had another class, but not for a few hours and he'd promised to meet Chloe for lunch in the student union.

As he turned, he hit his leg on the corner of the desk and hissed in pain.

"Son of a—"

He bit down on his lip before the curse word could sneak out in front of his students. *Damn, that hurt.*

"Guess you really did crash the bike," a familiar voice said behind him.

Gage gritted his teeth against the sharp sting in his calf. His leg was healing up fine, but it was still bandaged and the flesh beneath tender.

When he had it under control, he turned to his student. "Zane, how can I help you?"

Zane had a backpack slung over one shoulder, watching him curiously. "You hid it well during class. Is it bad?"

Gage shook his head. "Just some road rash."

Zane nodded. "Well, I don't know if you're going to be up for it, but I wanted to let you know that I go rock climbing at the indoor sport complex all the time. So, I could help get you all set up if you wanted to do that for the next article?"

Gage almost rejected the idea out of hand, but Zane was one of those challenging students: crazy smart but not entirely motivated. It concerned Gage a little, truthfully. Zane had been a model student in Communications 101 the year before.

Now that he'd made it into some of the more interesting journalism courses, he was missing assignments and showing up late.

Maybe letting him do this would get him more engaged in the class. Besides, if Zane had experience, maybe Gage could avoid another stupid accident.

"Okay," he said. "This weekend?"

Zane grinned wide. "I'm free Saturday afternoon."

"I'd go in with you, but I've already made an appointment for Bruiser," Ben told his mother as he pulled into the drop-off lane at the doctor's office. "You'll be okay on your own, right?"

The battered stray cat yowled unhappily from his cat carrier strapped into the back seat.

Ben looked over his shoulder. "I'm not very happy either, buddy," he said, before scowling down at the fresh scratches raking both arms.

Just as he'd suspected, getting Bruiser out from under the bed and into the carrier had been a battle. Bruiser had used his claws without remorse.

"I'll be fine, but I don't know why you're keeping that fleabag," his mom said.

He shrugged, a half smile pulling at his lips. "He just needs a little help. Maybe one day he'll be the picture of dignified house cat."

They both turned to look at Bruiser critically. His hair was matted, but that could be fixed. One ear was ragged, with a chunk missing, and a sour expression rested on his lopsided face.

"Or not," they both said and laughed.

"Jinx!" His mom said and pinched his bicep.

"Ow, dang, you haven't gotten me that good since I turned 11."

Ben wasn't dumb. He knew his mom was deflecting. He turned serious eyes on her, and her smile faded. He could see the worry lurking in her brown eyes.

"You sure you don't want me to come in? I know you're more comfortable when I can interpret the jargon. I can reschedule Bruiser."

She patted his knee and opened the car door

"Don't be silly. You can't leave him in the car. I'll be fine. Besides, like you said, my symptoms could mean a lot of things. Right?"

He nodded, and she got out of the car with a wave.

"Good luck with that mangy cat," she teased. "Oh, and before I forget, Karen's gay nephew is in town next week."

He groaned. "Mom, you promised no more set-ups."

"Yes, dear, but that was before you got so lonely you started taking in grumpy old tomcats."

He grimaced. "Bye, mom. You're gonna be late."

She smiled and closed the door, and he pulled out of the drop-off lane to head down the street to the vet's office.

As annoying as she was, his mom's heart was in the right place. And she might not be entirely wrong. He *was* lonely. But a date with a stranger he knew nothing about wasn't the answer any more than Bruiser was. At least Bruiser wouldn't leave him.

Another angry yowl erupted in the backseat.

Then again, he probably would if he could.

Gage met Chloe at the student union for a quick bite before her next class started. There was no formal cafeteria, with it being a junior college, just an area where you could pick up sandwiches and salads. Gage grabbed his usual roast beef, and joined Chloe's table as far from the groups of chattering students as she could manage.

"What have I told you about putting baby in the corner?" he teased.

She glanced up from her phone, where she'd been absorbed in texting. "God, you're old. No one quotes 'Dirty Dancing' anymore."

He shrugged and sank down in a plastic chair. A shaft of sunlight poured through the windows right into his eyes, so he looked down and concentrated on unwrapping his sandwich and taking a bite. Roast beef and melted gouda tangoed on his tongue, and he wolfed down another bite, suddenly ravenous. It was a good sandwich, but for $6, it should be.

"Slow down before you choke," Chloe said. Then smirked. "And speaking of choking ..."

He glanced up, squinting against the sunlight to see Chloe's face. "Another crappy rehearsal last night?"

"Well, yeah. I'm not panicking yet. We're pretty much always crap until rehearsal week, and then it all comes together. Don't believe anyone who tells you miracles don't happen. It's a miracle every damn season that I don't cancel the show out of sheer embarrassment."

Gage laughed. "Would never happen."

"True," she said breezily, "the show must go on. Even bad shows."

She gave a mock shudder and stabbed a bite of her club salad. "No, by choking, I meant you and that cute nurse."

She swooped her arm down and opened her fist wide, making a bombing noise.

"Thanks for that lovely illustration of me crashing and burning," he said dryly. "I might have needed that *except I was there.*"

Chloe chuckled unrepentantly, enjoying his humiliation at

the hands of the ER nurse. With the wiping out on a motorcycle, getting laughed at by a bunch of bikers and crashing with Ben, it had been a gold star day for mortification.

"Sorry," Chloe said, though she didn't sound all that sorry. "You need to get out more. Hit the clubs and get you some."

Gage glanced over his shoulder, making sure there were no students in eavesdropping range. That would be just what he needed. Those kids were like sharks smelling blood if you had a weakness. They'd be razzing him all hour instead of listening to what he had to say.

There were a few tables between them and the next set of students, and he didn't think any of them were in his classes, but he still lowered his voice.

"First of all, there are no gay clubs in Ashe, and I don't have the time or energy to drive all the way to Wichita on a regular basis. Most of those guys just want a hook-up anyway. Been there, done that, got the T-shirt."

She grinned. "Now, I want to see that outfit."

He ignored her. "The thing is, I'm over it. I'm never going to fall in love over a bathroom blowjob—"

"Do you guys really do that?" she interrupted. "That's not an exaggeration that's made in movies or books?"

He shrugged. "Depends on the type of bar."

"Have *you* done it?"

"Focus on the point, Chloe. I'm not interested in quick, messy hook-ups."

"Well, you're never going to meet the one if the only place you run into cute gay guys is the ER. That's seriously dangerous to your health."

He tossed a balled up napkin at her, and she dodged, chuckling.

"You're enjoying this way too much. That nurse crushed my ego."

She snorted. "Not possible."

"Yeah, I know. What was his problem anyway? How could he turn down all of this?" he said, gesturing toward his body.

She rolled her eyes. "Impossible to imagine."

Gage was kidding, but he knew he had a good body, especially for a college instructor. He'd gotten his share of admiring looks around campus, but he was careful not to engage with any students. It wasn't really *against* the rules, at least not if they weren't attending his classes, but he had no desire to date someone so young and unsettled.

He'd stopped casual hook-ups for a reason: Gage was ready to settle down. Finding a man who wanted to do the same was the tricky part. He hadn't quite figured out how to do that, and was just waiting for *love to find him*, like in those sappy romances Chloe read.

He didn't hold out much hope of it working. But he hadn't had much luck in trying to force relationships out of guys he met at the bar, either. Gage always rushed things and set off guys' alarm bells. Logically, he knew it was just his past messing with him. When you have a history of bouncing from foster family to foster family, you either withdraw completely or grab onto people so tight you suffocate them.

Gage popped the last bite of his sandwich in his mouth and started gathering up their trash. He assumed the conversation was over, but Chloe could be stubborn when she wanted something.

"I'm serious, Gage. You need to get out more. Come hang with me and some of the cast this week. We're going out after our next rehearsal, and I know we'll be ready to throw back a few. It's not a gay bar, but you need to socialize—"

"I socialize."

"Outside of the classroom," she said. "Preferably with liquor."

When he didn't answer, she batted her eyelashes. "Pretty please with a cherry on top?"

He smirked. "I may be hard up, but I'm not so virginal there will be any cherries involved."

"Ga-age," she whined. "Stop avoiding."

Huffing out a breath, he gave in like she knew he would.

"Okay, fine. But if it's awful, I get to duck out early."

She nodded eagerly, and he held up a finger to forestall her excitement.

"And you're not allowed to leave with some guy if I don't have a chance in hell of meeting anyone."

She grinned. "You drive a hard bargain, but you have a deal. No picking up unless you do."

Considering they'd be going not only to a straight bar, but one likely to be filled with students so close to the college, they were both pretty much guaranteed to go home alone.

But that was okay. He and his right hand had gotten used to their privacy anyway.

Ben rolled into the parking lot to pick up his mom an hour later, relieved to be through with the ordeal at the vet's office. He'd come through it with two new scratches to the top of his hands, but not as many as the vet tech, bless her heart.

By the time they left, Bruiser had been a sullen, silent weight in his carrier, too exhausted for any more theatrics. Or maybe just happy to leave the evil place with prodding fingers and sharp needles. He had all his shots now and a prescription for worms. Next, Ben would have to take him in for neutering.

Poor guy. At least he was being well fed. Or would be, as soon as Ben got to the store and purchased the dry cat food the veterinarian had recommended. Apparently tuna out of a can wasn't the ideal everyday meal, though Bruiser had seemed to enjoy it well enough.

He'd had just enough time to run Bruiser home, where he'd cautiously opened the cat carrier and jumped back, in fear of reprisal. The cat streaked by him, a scolding yowl echoing in his wake. He made straight for the bedroom, where Ben suspected he'd remain under the bed until food called him out.

He would feel sorrier for him, but those scratches stung.

Now, as he waited for his mom to come out, he allowed himself to think about what she might have learned in the doctor's office. Despite her tendency to over-react about her health she wasn't getting any younger. There would come a day she needed more than placating. A day when she was diagnosed with diabetes or heart disease or any number of potential conditions.

She opened the car door and slid in, and he turned toward her. "Well?"

She beamed a smile at him, to his great surprise. Usually doctor's visits left her stressed and confused, certain she was misunderstanding some vital piece of information that would ensure her good health.

"You were right," she said, patting his arm. "Just a kidney infection. So silly of me!"

"Really?" he said, surprised.

Some of his mom's anxiety must have rubbed off on him, because he wasn't expecting such a simple cut-and-dry answer.

She nodded, still smiling. "Just some antibiotics and I'm back in working order."

"Huh," he said, dumbfounded. "But you didn't have pain with urination first? Or a urinary tract infection?"

She laughed him off, shaking her head. "You of all people know how I get, Ben," she said. "I was so busy fretting that I overlooked the simplest explanation. I did notice I was dehydrated and experiencing some discomfort. I took some cranberry pills and drank some water the other day."

"Mom," he said, exasperated. "You know that if you have an actual infection, that won't cure it."

"I know, I know. I was just hoping to avoid the hassle of a doctor's visit," she said. "I know how you worry."

He opened his mouth to protest. He wasn't the one that worried. She worried. She'd thought she had pancreatic cancer, for God's sake. And all over a kidney infection.

But as her news sank in, he could breathe a bit easier. Maybe he worried more than he ever realized, and maybe she saw more than he'd thought.

Instead of arguing, he smiled. "Well, that's good news then. Let's run to the pharmacy."

He finger-combed his windblown hair and frowned at the empty window frame in his driver-side door. "After that, I need to get this window replaced. You want to come along for that?"

"Sure, sounds good. How's Bruiser?"

"Less happy than you are," Ben said, "but he'll live."

3

Ben let Alex guilt him into going out to a bar Thursday night.

She worked the day shift, but it was Ben's day off – and also the only evening they could feasibly go out together, given their work schedules.

He wasn't really in the mood to go out, and Alex had been irritating the crap out of him with all her biker boyfriend nonsense. Truth was, though, he was beginning to feel like a hermit. He hadn't gotten out of the house much since his break with Tripp, outside of regular lunch dates with his mother. Even before that, his dates with Tripp had been infrequent and unsatisfying – a prelude to sex and nothing more.

That was just a little sad.

"I may not be good company," he said, dragging his feet as they entered the bar where they were meeting a few other nurses and interns on staff.

When you worked at a hospital, you tended to socialize mostly with co-workers because no one else worked your crazy hours.

"Well, cheer up, Buttercup!" Alex said with a wide grin. "You need to get out more."

Ben snorted. "Yeah, because a straight bar is going to do a lot for me," he said, as they made their way up to the bar to get a drink. "And you're single too."

Alex wedged herself in next to him, elbowing aside a large guy who gave her an irritated look before shuffling over. His eyes skated over her bottom and he shrugged, as if he were thinking, *worth it.*

Ben did his best to keep a straight face.

"At least I'm getting out there and trying," Alex said, "and I'm not half the catch you are."

"Stop right there, Alex. Don't you dare sell yourself short."

She smiled. "You're right. I'm fabulous."

"Damn straight."

"But so are you."

"Not so straight," he deadpanned.

She giggled and shoved his shoulder. "Buy me a drink, dork."

Gage cast a look at the table, already starting a collection of empty shot glasses, and decided to get a pitcher of beer before these youngsters drank themselves to death.

Most junior college kids were too young to drink, but there were always a few nontraditional students. Tonight, Chloe had wrapped up a good rehearsal and demanded that he join her and a few of the play's cast members for a celebratory drink.

That drink had turned into many more, but they were all having a good time.

Gage knew Adam from one of his own classes. The guy was 24 or 25, a late starter but still young enough to build a career in his prime. The rest of the crowd he'd met only through Chloe, which was just as well. Gage didn't want too many of his own students to see him drinking, even if he was taking it slow compared to everyone else at the table.

He excused himself and headed for the bar. His eyes were casually scanning the crowd lined up for drinks when he spotted him.

Nurse Hotness.

If Ben had looked good in loose-fitting scrubs, he was damn near irresistible in snug jeans and a T-shirt. Gage greedily drank in the details he hadn't been able to make out in the hospital: long legs, perky ass, a body that filled out his T-shirt, suggesting more muscle than he would have expected on that slender frame.

As he watched, Ben picked up a pitcher and a couple of glasses. Worried he might miss his chance to reconnect, Gage slid up next to him.

"Need a hand?"

Ben turned, a polite refusal already leaving his lips before recognition lit his eyes. "Thanks, but I got it. ... Hey, it's you!"

"It's me," Gage agreed with a grin.

Ben's eyes panned down Gage's faded blue jeans. "How's the leg holding up?"

"It's holding up well enough for a dance. What do you say?"

"Um ..."

A round, friendly face appeared over his shoulder. "He says yes."

"Alex," he said, "you can't carry all these glasses."

"Dance with the handsome man, Ben."

"No, he's right," Gage said, sensing a polite rejection coming his way. He wasn't giving up yet, but he wanted to head off any attempt to get rid of him. "Let me help."

He grabbed the pitcher before Ben could protest and

followed a grinning Alex to a table full of women he soon learned were other nurses. Plus one intern with dark rings under her eyes who looked like she should be catching up on sleep instead of drinking, but everyone has their priorities.

He noticed Ben was the only man with the group.

"Drink up now, ladies," Alex crowed, "because soon you'll all be buying me a round. I am so winning the ER boyfriend pool."

"For fuck's sake," Ben muttered. "She's not even drunk yet."

"What's the ER boyfriend pool?"

Ben busied himself pouring beers for the nurses, but Alex was happy to fill in Gage. She grabbed her beer glass and took a big gulp before turning to Gage.

"Well, you see, honey, Ben's ex told him that he'd meet the one—"

"Alex!" Ben hissed.

"You know," she said, "his next great love—"

Ben grabbed Gage's hand and tugged him away from the table. "You know what? You want to dance? Let's dance."

Gage was curious about the whole ex-boyfriend story. Who wouldn't be? He wanted to know how recent the ex, and whether Ben still loved him, and if he had a shot with Ben despite his spectacular rejection at the ER.

But more than that, he wanted a chance to get his hands on the nurse. He was more than happy to dance with him, even if it was mostly an escape plan. Luckily, the bar was close to the college and there were always a few same-sex couples in the mix. They didn't have to worry about standing out too much or inciting any confrontations.

Ben led him into the center of the dance floor, so they were blocked on all sides by other couples, and grabbed Gage's shoulders. He kept plenty of space between them, but Gage grabbed his waist and tugged him a little closer. Nothing too indecent but close enough he could smell his subtle spicy cologne and the underlying antiseptic scent that lingered from the hospital even now. It wasn't unpleasant; somehow the smells worked to merge Ben's two identities: sweet nurse and vital man.

"Sorry about all that," Ben murmured close to his ear.

His breath fanned over the side of Gage's neck, sending tingles in all directions. Gage suppressed a shiver.

"No problem. I know all about nosy friends."

Which reminded him that he'd ditched his. He took a quick glance over Ben's shoulder, scanning the bar. It helped that he was a head taller than most everyone else on the dance floor. He spotted Chloe and the gang, and they were drinking and laughing, so they must have figured out he wasn't returning with a pitcher.

Oops.

Ben chuckled. "Sometimes I want to kill her, but she's got a good heart."

"Yeah, she seems sweet."

"Ha, no. She's evil," Ben said. "But she loves me, and she's a life-saver at work. I could just do without all the interest in my love life. Sometimes I feel like a damn project. Look at Ben, the fixer-upper. He must be desperate for a boyfriend!"

Gaged snorted. "You're anything but a fixer-upper."

Ben drew back a little to look at him. "How would you know? We just met."

Gage didn't mean to raise Ben's hackles. He smoothed a hand up and down his spine, subconsciously trying to soothe him.

"You're right," he acknowledged, "but you look like the whole package to me. You're hot. You've got a good career. You've got friends."

He pulled back to grin down at Ben, who was already blushing. *So sweet.*

"I could extoll some of your other virtues, but I don't want to get slapped."

Ben's lips curled up. "There's little chance of that."

Gage took in the spark of heat in his eyes and the flush in his cheeks. He tugged him a little closer, and Ben pressed against him.

With their friends on either ends of the bar, mostly forgotten, they danced.

A couple of hours later, Ben was flushed with heat inside and out. The surface of his skin crackled with each brush of contact against Gage, and he couldn't shut down the fantasies of what it would be like to get him out of his clothes and inside Ben's body.

Gage spoke into his ear. "Want to get out of here?"

Ben's heart flipped in his chest. *Hell, yes!*

He might not trust himself to date Gage, but hooking up with the gorgeous man? Perfect solution.

It had been a long damn time since he had sex, and he was craving Gage in the worst way. He wasn't eager to start another fuck buddy situation, but he could handle a hook-up. He'd had a few before Tripp came along, and they'd never left him shattered the way relationships did.

He nodded, a small smile tugging at his lips. "I thought you'd never ask."

"Oh, I'm asking," Gage said, his lips grazing Ben's cheek as he spoke.

Ben couldn't wait for that mouth to make contact with his. Preferably somewhere other than a straight bar.

Gage grabbed his hand and tugged him through the crowd toward a crowded table in the corner. "Just gotta grab my jacket and keys."

They'd been dancing ever since Ben dragged him from Alex's table, stopping only once to grab some water and take a breather. They'd taken their time-out with the gaggle of nurses because they were closer, but Ben had shot fire out of his eyes at Alex and told her to zip her lips. Amazingly, she'd agreed, and they'd joked and laughed about general ER chaos and grumbled about entitled doctors.

To his surprise, Gage had chimed in about the doctor who treated him.

"What's the deal with Dr. Johnston?" he'd asked.

"He's a creep," Dawn volunteered with a shudder. As everyone turned to look at her, she blushed. "Oops, did I say that out loud? He's a professional, Dr. Johnston. Very thorough in his exams."

"What happened?" Alex said.

She sounded far less drunk than earlier. A veneer of professionalism dropped over her in an instant.

Dawn's eyes widened. "Nothing with me," she insisted. "I wouldn't be his type."

Her eyes flicked to Ben, and suddenly everyone stared at him.

"What? Nothing happened with me, either."

"He was pretty interested in your ass when he treated me," Gage volunteered, and Ben gaped at him.

"No," he said weakly. "I'm sure it just looked that way. Dr. Johnston and I have *never*—"

Gage dropped a hand to his knee and squeezed it reassuringly. "I didn't say you were interested in him."

"So, what did happen? Are you just speculating, Dawn?" Alex asked. "Being attracted to Ben doesn't automatically equate to being a creep."

"I certainly hope not," Gage mumbled under his breath, and Ben smiled.

The hand on his knee was a heavy warmth, and he silently willed it to move up his thigh. But Gage wasn't a creep, and he hadn't gotten too handsy yet, even on the dance floor. *God, he wanted him to get handsy.*

"No, not Ben," Dawn said. "I saw him hit on a patient. A young patient," she said, looking uncomfortable.

"A male patient?" Alex asked.

"Not that it matters," Ben interjected. "Male or female, a young patient shouldn't be dealing with that. The question we should be asking is: how young?"

Alex nodded. "Ben's right."

Dawn shrugged. "I don't remember the exact age. Maybe 18 or 19?"

"So, an adult?" Ben said, relieved.

It wasn't good. It wasn't professional. But it wasn't pedophilia, thank heavens.

"I think so," Dawn said, not sounding sure at all. "Definitely in the teens, at least."

Alex groaned. "I'm going to have to report this. You should have come to me right away."

Dawn looked uncomfortable. "I wasn't 100 percent sure of what I saw. I'm still not," she said hurriedly.

Ben turned to Gage. He was getting far too much insider drama. This kind of personnel matter shouldn't even be discussed among all the nurses who were present, much less someone not even employed by the hospital.

"Another dance?" he'd asked.

Gage had agreed easily enough, and they'd danced long enough to put the matter entirely out of Ben's mind. In fact, there was only one thing on his mind at this point: getting naked with a hot man.

It had been too long. He wasn't a slut by any stretch of the imagination, but he usually had a regular sex partner.

Ben followed Gage to the table where he'd left his own group of friends, content to go with the flow. As long as the flow took him straight into Gage's pants.

He didn't even care that he was ditching out on Alex. She deserved it for trying to flaunt his failed love life in front of Gage. He knew she was trying to help, but damn, he wouldn't mind if Gage never heard that story.

He wouldn't have shared it with Alex if he knew she was going to tease him with it for weeks on end. It was her way of turning a painful thing into a joke, he knew. That was how the nurses handled the terrible things they saw, with twisted humor. But he wasn't ready to laugh about Tripp yet.

Ben almost shot down Gage to avoid feeding the flames of Alex's enthusiasm, but then he'd taken another look at him — strong and broad and tall, and so warm and friendly at the same time — and decided a night with him would definitely be worth the teasing.

As they approached Gage's table, Ben recognized the friend who'd picked him up at the ER. There were about five other people crowded around a table cluttered with empty glasses, and every one of them was watching their approach.

As soon as they were within earshot, they started in.

"Mr. Evans is getting laid tonight!"

That was followed by cackling laughter and wolf whistles. Gage cringed, and Ben grinned to see red crawling up his neck.

"Knock it off, guys."

"Yeah, how come we go to a straight bar and he's the one to get laid?" someone grumbled.

"Shit, so much for that bet that he and Chloe were secretly getting it on."

"Adam!" Chloe protested. "I can do better, thank you."

"Love you too, sweetheart," Gage said dryly.

"Oh, get out of here. You bagged your hot nurse, so you got nothing to cry about."

Gage laughed and hugged Chloe goodbye, grabbed his leather jacket — a new one, by the looks of it — and slid an arm around Ben's waist, as if he were worried he might escape. If he'd wanted to run, he would have done it by now.

"Bye-bye, Nurse Ben," Chloe trilled as they walked away.

"Tap that ass!" someone called out, with more laughter.

Gage turned back. "You're not in high school anymore, guys!"

They left to a chorus of "oooohs" as they stepped out the door. Once outside, Gage turned to Ben.

"Sorry about all that."

"Forget it," Ben said. "Just get me someplace private so I can kiss you already."

"God, yes," Gage said fervently, sucking in his bottom lip, which only served to tantalize Ben more. "Your place or mine?"

Ben's initial instinct was to choose Gage's place. That way he could escape without having to kick Gage out, which was kind of a dick thing to do.

"Yours would be ... oh, shit. Bruiser."

"Bruiser?"

"My cat. We better go to my place. I just got him recently, and he's still settling in. He's a little wild."

"Like feral?"

Ben, losing patience, grabbed Gage's arms. "I'm going to be feral if you don't get me in bed soon."

Gage laughed, but there was a rough edge to his voice. "I might like that."

Ben hip-checked him and headed for his car. "Follow me over. I live on Grand."

"Don't try to lose me, Nurse Hotness."

Ben laughed. "Nurse Hotness, really?"

"It's what I called you in my head that night at the ER," Gage said with a shrug and a grin.

Ben's chest went warm, and he turned away.

Do not let your stupid feelings get in on this action. This is about your body and nothing else.

―――――

They didn't make it inside.

Gage followed Ben up a walkway and onto a small porch. He lived in half of a duplex, but it looked like a cute little bungalow from what Gage could see of it in the darkness.

Ben pulled out his keys to open the door, immediately dropped them and turned to Gage with a flustered expression.

One look at his dark eyes and flushed skin, and Gage was done.

He grabbed Ben's face and pulled him in for a kiss.

The angle was all wrong. Ben was only half-turned toward him, and their lips were off-center, but it was still the best kiss he'd had in a long time. Ben's lips were hot and moist and just as plump as he'd imagined.

Ben twisted in his arms, breaking the kiss only to come back at a better angle, and Gage pushed him up against his door.

Their mouths crashed together hot and wet and sloppy, but Gage didn't care about the lack of finesse because heat was searing through his body, not just his groin but rushing through his bloodstream and out to each and every limb.

He wanted this man with a desperation that surprised him.

Ben pushed him back, gasping for breath.

"Keys," he said, and Gage suddenly remembered they were on the porch, possibly giving the neighbors a show.

He eased back to give Ben room to lean down and grab them, waiting impatiently as Ben unlocked the door.

Then they were inside, and Gage lost no time pushing Ben up against the other side of his door. He pressed his body against him, reveling in the feel of Ben's chest and thighs and oh yes ... the hard ridge of his cock.

They kissed for several long moments, their frantic clash easing into an exploration. Tongues met and curled, sliding against each other. Ben's lips softened against his, caressing with soft glides.

Gage rocked his hips, grinding against Ben until he moaned and broke the kiss to gasp out one word: "Bedroom."

"Lead the way."

He stepped back, and then startled as a loud yowl rent the air. "What the—"

"Bruiser!"

Ben darted around him and grabbed up an ugly fur ball with tattered ... everything.

"Poor baby. Let me get you some food."

Gage's eyebrows went up. "You feed him this late at night?"

Ben glanced back as he carried Bruiser toward the kitchen. Gage followed, hoping the cat didn't prove to be a cock-blocker for much longer. He'd come so close to his fantasy he could almost taste it.

Not that Ben was just a fantasy. He was very real.

"I work the late shift, so somehow we just got into that pattern," Ben answered as he deposited Bruiser in front of a food dish, and grabbed a scoop of dry cat food to pour into the bowl. He stuck the scoop back in the bag in the pantry, and turned to Gage.

"There!" he said, and promptly launched himself at Gage.

Gage stumbled back a step as Ben's weight crashed into him, and they laughed breathily together before Ben latched onto his throat and the only sound Gage made was a drawn out moan.

"I love your stubble," Ben breathed, rasping his hand over it.

"I love your everything," Gage muttered.

"Well, let's go love our things in the bedroom," Ben said with a wide smile.

"Hell, yeah."

4

Bringing Gage into his bedroom was a surreal feeling.

On the one hand, he'd brought plenty of hook-ups home before. On the other, he'd never hooked up with a patient before, and as much as this was just a one-night stand, he couldn't help the feeling he knew Gage in a way he hadn't known any of those past sex partners.

Except for Tripp, but it was weeks into their fling before Tripp came to his house.

He hastily shoved away memories of his ex in favor of focusing on the sexy man unbuttoning his shirt. Gage was more lean than Tripp, but he was damn sexy, with the best abs of any teacher Ben had ever laid eyes on.

"I am so hot for teacher right now," Ben said, then laughed. "I've always wanted to say that."

Gage grinned as he shrugged out of his shirt. "Good, because I've been hot for nurse since the moment I saw you."

Ben grabbed his T-shirt and pulled it over his head, and they came together for another kiss before separating to tug off their jeans and fall into bed.

He already knew what he wanted, but he wasn't sure if Gage would be on the same page. He couldn't read him.

"Condoms and lube in the drawer, if you want ..."

"God, yes," Gage said. "But first, roll over."

He pushed Ben onto his stomach. *Rude.*

Maybe it was just a hook-up, but Gage didn't have to make it so obvious he didn't want to watch Ben's face while they fucked. *What happened to being Nurse Hotness?*

His chest clenched, and he tried to will the feeling away. *You always do this. He's not making love to you, so who cares?*

"As a nurse, you're always taking care of people," Gage said, as he leaned over him, pressing a kiss to the back of his neck.

"Mmm." Ben hummed, agreeing without speaking.

"Tonight's different. Tonight, I'm going to take care of you."

Gage laid his hands on Ben's shoulders and began to massage. Ben's eyes closed involuntarily as his body relaxed under those talented hands. As he worked over Ben's body, Gage leaned in to press small kisses along his upper back and neck — a highly erogenous zone for Ben.

He shivered as a chill rushed over his skin.

"I want you to feel better than you've ever felt before," Gage murmured, before pressing a kiss even lower, on his tailbone.

Ben's heart sped up, his body thrumming with anticipation. As Gage moved on to massaging his glutes, he groaned.

"I knew your ass would be perfect."

Ben sucked in a breath and pushed his ass back into Gage's hands.

"Touch me," he demanded.

Gage was doing nothing but touching Ben, but he seemed to understand. He eased back and nudged Ben to turn over.

Something settled inside him when they were face to face once again. Gage hadn't been treating him like a meaningless hook-up at all. More like a boyfriend, which was concerning in a whole other way. Ben was in a Catch-22: He wanted to matter, but he didn't want to get too invested. He'd done that too many times before.

Gage's hand wrapped around his aching cock, and Ben pushed away his thoughts.

It was a one-time thing, and he wanted to enjoy it, not analyze it. As he shuddered under Gage's touch, he felt the last of his hesitation drop away.

He knew how to do this part. He was *good* at this part.

Gage kept his grip loose and stroked too slowly to get Ben anything but more turned on. He huffed a frustrated breath.

"What do you want?" Gage asked.

"You inside me," Ben said without hesitation. "Condoms and lube are—"

"In the nightstand. Yeah, you told me." Gage chuckled. "I like a man who knows what he wants."

"I mean, unless you want to bottom? I'm flexible."

"I bet you are," Gage said with a grin. "No, I'm fine topping. I have a feeling you're going to be a bossy bottom anyway."

Ben laughed. "Shut up and fuck me."

"See? I knew it."

Gage knew Ben expected him to grab the condom and go to town, but he wanted to make this last a bit longer. He was eager to be inside of Ben, but once he was, the finish line would rush at him in record time.

Instead of reaching for the condoms, he slid down the bed, getting up-close and personal with Ben's cock. It matched Ben's body perfectly: slender, well-formed, flushed with desire.

Gage let his gaze pan up.

He mentally added another adjective: strong.

Everything about Ben was so warm, he'd almost expected him to be soft when the scrubs came off. A little fragile, perhaps, to match the vulnerability that came into his eyes when Gage asked him why they couldn't date.

Thank God, he'd broken through those defenses.

In truth, Ben didn't have the body of a gym rat or even an athlete. There were no washboard abs or bulging muscles, but as Gage ran his hands up the body before him, admiring with his sense of touch as well as sight, Ben's belly was firm and his chest was solid.

His shoulders weren't especially broad, but Ben was no twink. His strength must come from good genes or a healthy lifestyle, or both.

"Gage, for fuck's sake," Ben muttered. "Are you trying to drive me crazy?"

He chuckled, letting his breath skate over Ben's cock. *Time to get to work.*

He'd figure out all the secrets to Ben's body eventually. Right now, the man vibrated with need, and Gage wanted more than anything to be the man who fulfilled Ben's needs.

He lowered his mouth, tracing his tongue around the head of Ben's cock.

Ben wasn't having it. Instead of complaining about the teasing touch, he thrust his hips up.

His cock pushed into the heat of Gage's mouth, going deep but not so deep as to choke him. Gage had pretty much mastered his gag reflex, but he hadn't yet relaxed his throat, so he was glad Ben reined himself in.

But now that he knew what Ben wanted, he set about preparing himself.

"No more teasing," Ben panted, thrusting his hips again.

This time, Gage moved his head down as Ben thrust up, taking his cock to the back of his throat.

The strangled moan that left Ben's lips was more than worth the slight burn of deep throating.

He stayed in that position, stuffed to the gills with cock, and worked his tongue along Ben's shaft inside his mouth.

One hand anchored Ben's hips, as he pulled up and began a quick suck-and-slide rhythm. He was taking control of this joy ride. With his other hand, he slid his fingers down, massaging Ben's balls and moving down, down, until a fingertip found his entrance.

Ben let out a litany of profanity. "Fuck fuck, yes, just like that. Fuucck. No, wait! Stop!"

Gage let Ben's cock slip from his mouth.

"Problem?" he asked, a little breathless from the blowjob.

"Yeah," Ben said, sitting up and reaching for the drawer in the bedside table. "I'm going to come, and that is *not* the plan."

"Funny, I thought that was exactly the plan."

Ben rolled his eyes and tossed the condom at Gage. "Suit up. It's time to fuck."

Gage laughed out loud.

He'd been right about Ben being bossy in bed, and he loved it. There was no sign of the hesitation he'd shown when Gage first clumsily hit on him. God, that had been lame. He was glad Ben had given him another chance because their chemistry was great.

He rolled on the condom, and Ben flipped open the lube, moving forward as if to pour it over Gage's cock.

Gage stopped him. "Hold up a sec. Let me do you first."

Ben raised an eyebrow. "I can do myself," he said. "I don't need much prep."

Gage shook his head. No way he was going to rush in and risk hurting Ben. Pain was not the name of the game tonight. Best sex ever was the goal, and he intended to surpass expectations.

"Please let me," he said, making sad eyes at Ben. "I like to do it."

Ben hesitated. "No more teasing?"

Gage crossed his heart with a finger. "I promise."

He grinned wickedly when Ben handed over the lube. "Now you're mine to do with as I please," he said, adding an evil laugh. "And I do ... so ... please."

He flicked his tongue out, licking up and down Ben's shaft in between words while he poured lube onto his fingers.

"Oh God, what have I done?" Ben gasped, laughter in his voice. "Don't go easy on me."

Gage circled a finger around Ben's hole while sucking the head of his cock. With a little pressure, his finger slid in, and they both moaned.

He raised his head. "Don't go easy?"

"Mmm-mmm," Ben said, which he interpreted to mean no. "Go hard. And fast. More fingers, now. Please, God."

His tone turned commanding, and Gage felt a surge of lust. An unraveling Ben was sexy as fuck.

He complied, pushing in a second finger. He pumped his fingers carefully, working them deeper. He reveled in the feel of Ben's body relaxing and opening up for him.

"Turn your fingers. ... Here, like this."

Ben grabbed his wrist and turned it, angling his fingers to hit his prostate. Then he pulled Gage's hand forward, taking his fingers in past the knuckle.

His fingertips grazed Ben's prostate, and the man groaned deep in his chest as his cock lurched. Gage took the hint and began finger fucking Ben more forcefully, making sure to nudge his prostate on each pass.

He was more amused than offended by Ben's actions, but he felt the need to defend his sexual prowess.

"I know you're a nurse, Ben, but I do actually know where the prostate is located."

Ben grunted. "Good, you can prove it with your cock. I'm ready."

Gage slid his fingers carefully from Ben's body and pushed his legs up to drape over his shoulders. Then he grabbed Ben's hips, tilting his ass up, and pressed his cock against his entrance.

He glanced down as he pushed forward, watching Ben's body stretch to accommodate him. He pushed slowly and steadily, waiting for that moment when Ben's muscles would transition from tense resistance to relaxed invitation.

Easy, Gage, he told himself, as tight heat enveloped his cock. The desire to pound the fuck out of Ben was strong, but he managed to hold back until he heard Ben's labored breathing catch and a moan of pleasure spill from his lips.

Then he surged forward, pushing deeper, and his own groan joined Ben's sounds of pleasure. He pulled back, almost to the point of leaving Ben's body, and surged forward again, hard.

"Fuck!" Ben shouted, scrabbling at his back to pull him in tighter.

He gripped Ben's hips harder, keeping him locked in place, as he finally gave in to his desire to fuck the hell out of Nurse Hotness.

He swiveled his hips, taking care to show Ben that he knew where to find his prostate, and was rewarded with more moans. Ben's voice was hoarse, a rougher version of his usual warm tones, and it amped up Gage's lust.

"You're sexy as fuck," he managed to get out between heaving breaths.

"You're the sexy one," Ben said, deflecting the compliment.

Gage wasn't sure why, but something about that small sign of insecurity made him slow down. Fucking Ben hard and fast would be satisfying, but he wanted to give Ben something more than that. He wanted to give him intimacy. Emotion.

He eased Ben's legs down and dropped his body down, holding himself up on his arms a hair's breadth from Ben's chest.

He leaned down to kiss Ben, and the man responded eagerly. As they kissed, Gage stopped moving, unable to coordinate fucking and making out at the same time. He lost himself in the feel of Ben's tongue and lips merging messily with his own.

He lifted his face to meet Ben's eyes.

"You're sexy," he repeated seriously. "Gorgeous and talented and probably out of my league."

Ben laughed, turning his head aside. A blush colored his cheeks, and Gage knew it had more to do with his words than sexual arousal.

He rocked his hips gently, dropping kisses along Ben's jaw and throat.

"I'm glad you gave me a chance," he whispered against the deliciously rough stubble under his lips.

Ben didn't answer. Instead he turned his head and kissed Gage hard before pushing him away. Gage's heart lurched, but before any true worry could take hold, Ben spoke.

"Lay down. It's my turn to be in charge."

Gage suppressed a laugh as he pulled out and dropped onto his back and crossed his arms behind his head. Ben had been in charge from the moment they met, but he wasn't about to tell him that.

He smirked. "Hey, if you want to do all the work, don't let me stop you."

"Good, I won't."

Ben straddled his body, moving one hand behind him to grasp Gage's cock and press it against his ass.

As with everything else in bed, Ben did not tease, even though he would have had just cause after Gage drew out foreplay. Instead, he pushed back, forcing his body to open and take Gage to the hilt, in one smooth action.

Gage groaned. "Holy fuck, Ben."

Ben smiled down at him. "Hold on, we're just getting started."

Then he began to move. And Jesus, that was an erotic sight. Ben's body was graceful and sinuous as he circled his hips and ground back on Gage's cock. His eyes dropped closed, dark lashes fanning against his skin, and he bit down on his bottom lip as little whimpering sounds gave away his pleasure.

It wasn't long before he'd set a fast pace, slamming back against Gage's cock. Taking it in hard strokes and grinding it against his prostate with a little twist of his hips. Watching him not just accept pleasure, but take it forcefully, was hot.

It wasn't as intimate as the love-making Gage had initiated, but it was phenomenal sex. Like the best fucking sex of his life phenomenal.

Gage watched the full-body flush move up Ben's torso in a wave as he got closer to orgasm. His hands clutched at Gage's chest, tangling in chest hair and digging almost painfully into his flesh, but it all added a nice edge to the pleasure cresting inside him.

Gage let his hands skate up Ben's flanks, exploring his body while Ben power bottomed. He enjoyed the freedom to touch more, letting Ben take control of his own pleasure. He massaged Ben's chest, pausing to tweak his nipples.

Judging by his reaction, Ben wasn't overly sensitive there, so he moved on, sliding his hands down to grab Ben's perfect ass.

That got more of a reaction.

His eyes slid open and he pressed back against Gage's hands, subtly asking for more. Gage squeezed his ass, massaging his glutes once more as he had during that rubdown that seemed hours ago now. He pulled Ben's cheeks apart and slid a finger down, circling around his own cock and the stretched ring of flesh around it.

Ben made a broken sound, collapsing forward against his chest. He hadn't come, but he was close enough he was trembling.

Gage grabbed Ben's hips and lifted him a few inches while he thrust his hips under him, fucking him as hard as he could in the position.

Ben breathed hard against his neck. His body was boneless against Gage, but his moans and whimpers told him Ben was right there on the edge with him.

"Touch yourself," Gage whispered into his ear.

Ben pushed a hand between their sweaty bodies, taking himself in hand. His breath grew harsher against Gage's neck, and then he exploded with a groan and rush of warm semen that overflowed his hand onto Gage's stomach.

Gage's grip tightened on Ben's hips as the man's inner muscles clutched and pulled at his cock. He managed another two thrusts and came hard in the condom, jerking as he pulsed inside Ben.

"Oh. My. God," Ben mumbled, as his body quivered with aftershocks.

Gage chuckled, his chest vibrating with his laugh under Ben. "Sounds about right."

Ben eased up on arms that were still fucking trembling — had the man turned all his muscles to jelly? — and collapsed onto the bed beside him.

He needed to shower and come up with a way to tell Gage to leave that wouldn't make him into a total ass. Right now, though, he needed to breathe and let his heart slow to a reasonable pace and process the shockwave that was his orgasm.

Not even with Tripp could he remember coming so hard. Or being so shaken his muscles turned to water.

Gage Evans was something else.

He was also uncharacteristically quiet.

Ben peeked at him from the corner of his eye, feeling vulnerable now that the sex had come and gone.

"Everything good?" he asked hesitantly

Gage rolled toward him and nuzzled his face into the space between Ben's shoulder and neck.

"Everything's great," he murmured. "Best sex ever."

Ben snorted skeptically, even though, yeah, it had been pretty amazing. Gage's blowjob skills were truly impressive, but he'd probably gone through a lot of sex partners to get that good. As had Ben. Neither of them were inexperienced.

Ben might not be able to hold onto a man, but he'd never had trouble getting sex. Bar hook-ups and friends with benefits had seen him through all the years since he'd experienced his first heartbreak at the hands of his college boyfriend.

Tripp wasn't even the primary reason he was so guarded about dating again. He'd just been the guy who had slipped past Ben's defenses and reminded him why he needed to keep that guard up. Colin got all the credit for Ben's wary nature.

He'd met Colin while in college. They'd had a biology class together, though Colin wasn't pursuing a degree in the field. He'd taken the class to fulfill a general education science credit while attending business school.

In retrospect, his attitude toward his chosen field should have been a red flag. Colin had big plans to move to New York and make heaps of money. He admired some of the most ruthless businessmen in America.

He was cute, though, and so smart. They'd fallen into bed

almost immediately, neither of them virgins, and they'd maintained no boundaries. They had class together; they had meals together; they slept in Ben's bed together since he had a roommate who was often at his girlfriend's place.

Until one day, he got a text from Colin.

It's been fun, but it's time to move on.

Ben had been sideswiped. He'd told Colin he loved him just days before.

Colin hadn't freaked out. He hadn't said it back, but he'd smiled and kissed Ben on the nose and told him he was so sweet he gave him a toothache. He'd figured Colin needed more time to confess his love, and he was fine with that.

Ben never once suspected Colin didn't care for him at all.

He'd been so naive. That text came the day after the end of the semester, the day after the one class they had together had ended.

Colin had brushed off his questions before blocking his number. He'd never come back to Ben's room, and Ben hadn't seen him on campus.

That was it. One text, and his heart had been torn apart.

"You didn't think it was great?" Gage asked, bringing him back to the present. *What were they talking about?* Oh yes, the best sex ever, according to Gage.

Ben was tempted to tease him, but the hint of worry in his voice kept Ben honest.

"Yeah, I did. Really great," he agreed.

So great, he was tempted to extend their one-time hook-up into a series of hook-ups. But he'd tried the friends with benefits situation with Tripp, and he knew he couldn't trust himself not to develop feelings if he was sleeping with a guy.

He forced himself to roll out of bed, desperate for a little distance. "I'm gonna grab a quick shower."

He didn't invite Gage to join him, quickly crossing to the

attached bathroom. He slipped inside and locked the door, needing the reassurance he really was alone for the next few minutes.

Taking a deep breath and releasing it, he willed himself to relax.

"It was just sex, Ben," he told himself as he turned on the shower and stepped inside. "The best sex ever," he admitted, now that Gage wouldn't hear him, "but just sex."

He scrubbed himself clean, taking care to remove all traces of semen and lube. Then he used the toilet, because it couldn't be avoided after bottoming.

Finally cleaned up and ready to return to the bedroom, he felt a flicker of guilt. He should have offered to clean up Gage before he came in, so he could leave if he wanted. He'd been in the bathroom twenty minutes at this point. Maybe Gage even thought he was avoiding him and had left.

The thought made his heart squeeze, even though it'd probably be for the best. He didn't want to hurt Gage's feelings. The man had been amazing — the perfect blend of sweet and sexy, rough and tender, playful and serious. Somehow they'd run the gamut of all those things in one bout of amazing sex.

Would it be that good a second time?

Ben shut down that thought. It wasn't going to happen again.

Taking a deep breath to brace himself for the unpleasant task of asking Gage to leave, he returned to the bedroom to find the man sound asleep in his bed.

"Gage?" he said quietly, just to make sure, but the man's eyelids didn't so much as flutter.

Ben noticed his lips were turned up in a satisfied smile.

The thought of waking him up to kick him out seemed heartless, and Ben's past experiences demonstrated he had too much heart rather than too little. He couldn't do it.

Fine. Just one night, and then he'd send him on his way in

the morning. It would be less awkward that way. They could part ways more gracefully, without it seeming as if Ben was kicking him out.

He walked around the bed and climbed in on his side. Gage was taking up a lot of the bed, so he nudged him in the hopes he'd move over. Instead, Gage pulled Ben against him, spooning around his body.

He couldn't deny it. It was kind of nice to cuddle with someone as he let his weariness wash over him and closed his eyes.

He'd distance himself tomorrow. Right now, he needed this more than he needed to protect himself.

5

Gage woke with a feeling of warm contentment. With a smile, he snuggled in deeper, rubbing his cheek against the pillow, until he realized part of that warmth came from another body.

His eyes snapped open as memories of the night before washed through him.

Ben.

Rumpled and bed-creased, he still looked gorgeous. He was also awake, watching Gage with a strange worry etched on his face.

They lay so close together, Gage could see the few freckles sprinkled over his nose that normally blended in with his warm skin tone.

With just an inch between them, it was the easiest thing in the world to bridge the gap and press a kiss to those sweet lips.

Gage was looking forward to a few long kisses, if not more, before he had to get ready for work. He wished fervently it was the weekend.

Ben went still, not responding to the kiss. Even worse, he turned away.

"I guess you probably want to get going. You have work, right?"

Gage heard the dismissal in his tone. Even though his internal clock was telling him he had plenty of time, he checked his phone on the table next to the bed. It read 6 a.m.

He took another look at Ben.

The man looked miserable. Way more tense than anyone who'd had such great sex the night before ought to be.

Gage hadn't missed the way Ben kept his distance after the orgasms had come and gone. He'd made a quick retreat to the shower, and Gage had waited patiently for his return — both hoping to get a turn to clean up and maybe a chance to chase that distant look from his eyes.

He must have fallen asleep before Ben returned.

It wasn't all that unusual to feel a little awkward after that level of intimacy the first time, but he suspected Ben's discomfort ran deeper.

"I've got time," Gage ventured. "We could have breakfast or whatever. I wouldn't say no to a few more kisses."

It seemed in bad taste to say he wouldn't mind a blowjob, but in fact, it sounded just about perfect.

Ben's expression closed down. Like last night, he rolled away, scooping up some boxer briefs from the floor and tugging them on.

"Last night was great," he said in a dead voice. "Thank you. But we both know it was a one-time thing."

Gage's heart stuttered.

"One-time thing?" he echoed.

Ben nodded. "We hooked up, and it was good. But you don't owe me anything."

Gage was stunned. Truly. Not that Ben wouldn't want a repeat. He'd hoped for more, but it's not like they'd laid out their plans the night before. No, he was more taken aback that Ben seemed to have convinced himself Gage didn't want anything more. That if he did, it only came out of a sense of obligation.

That couldn't be further from the truth.

"Ben," he said in exasperation, "I know we didn't make any promises, but I like you."

To his disappointment, Ben grabbed a T-shirt instead of answering. He pulled it on as if it were armor against Gage's words.

Feeling off-balance, Gage slipped out of bed and pulled on his briefs. He spoke without looking at Ben, certain he wouldn't enjoy his expression right now.

Ben still hadn't said anything, and Gage was growing frustrated. "I asked you out that night at the ER, and not for a hookup. I thought maybe we could date. I like you."

He thought Ben was going to freeze him out, but after a long moment, he responded.

"You don't know me."

"Not very well," Gage admitted, and Ben's gaze darted to his in surprise before skittering away. "That's the point of dating, actually. To get to know each other, to see if we might want to explore a relationship."

Ben dropped down, perching on the edge of the bed, and Gage joined him. Finally, Ben met his eyes.

"Dating an adrenaline addict is not on my list of things to do," he said. "I know the initial rush of meeting someone can be thrilling, but the thrill wears off."

Not this again?

"I'm not an adrenaline addict, but even if I were. ... Are you saying guys who ride motorcycles or climb mountains are incapable of love and commitment?"

"No, of course not, but it takes someone more exciting than me to hold their interest. I'm not enough to—"

"Stop right there." Gage grasped Ben's face, tilting his head to look into his eyes. "You're enough. You're more than enough. I don't know who hurt you to damage your self-esteem this way—"

Ben laughed. "I don't have low self-esteem. I'm just honest with myself. I'm boring. I like quiet nights in. I'm not a risk-taker."

"No kidding."

Ben bristled. "See? You don't like that about me!"

"Only because it keeps you from giving me a chance! Jesus, Ben, we were so fucking good together last night. Tell me I'm not alone in believing that, because that would taint the whole experience."

Ben looked torn about his answer, but eventually nodded. "It was great, but it was just sex. You wanted me, and you got me. Now that I'm out of your system, you can move on."

Gage groaned in frustration. *Why did this always happen to him?* He'd meet a guy, and invariably he wanted more and the guy didn't. The harder he pushed, the more the other guy resisted, until the whole experience left a bad taste in his mouth.

He didn't want that with Ben. He had been so certain it would be different this time, especially after the dancing and the flirting and the mind-blowing sex.

Ben was so much more than a random hook-up. He never imagined this would be their after-sex glow.

He kissed Ben hard, pouring his desire into it. Giving it one last-ditch effort.

"There's no out of my system. You're not some craving for ice cream. If you gave me a chance—"

Ben was already shaking his head. "Please don't make this harder," he whispered.

"Tell me who hurt you," Gage said, feeling desperate. "I'll kick his ass for making you believe you're not worthy of anything you want."

"It's not his fault. We were just fuck buddies. I wanted more, but he met someone else and fell in love."

He shrugged a shoulder as if it was no big deal, but Gage saw the pain underneath.

"Ben," he said gently, "maybe he just wasn't the man for you."

"He's not the first. I attract men who like to hook up, but they don't stick around. I'm tired of fighting it."

"Maybe I want to stick around."

"You say that now, but you won't be the one cleaning up the mess when it doesn't work out. So thanks, but no thanks, Gage."

Ben stood and crossed to the door. Gage jumped up, hoping to catch him before he stormed out.

"Wait, Ben. For fuck's— ow, shit!"

Ben turned, eyes wide. "Bruiser! No. Bad kitty!"

Two paws had stretched out from under the bed and clawed the shit out of his bare ankle. Looking down, Gage saw he had angry scratches on both sides of his left leg. Thank fuck, the cat couldn't reach his healing road rash.

He jumped out of reach as the paws released and came back for a second attack. A disturbingly dark yowl came from under the bed, and Gage backed away another step.

"I'm so sorry, Gage. Are you okay?"

"Fine," he said gruffly, moving around the room to gather up the rest of his belongings. He tugged on clothes and shoes as he went, and pocketed his cellphone and wallet.

"I'm sorry."

He looked up to see Ben watching him with concern. He was worried about the damage his cat had done when it was his rejection that stung. Now that he'd had a few minutes to process, Gage's pride hurt.

And so did his ankle. *Fuck.*

"You weren't kidding when you said he was feral."

Ben winced. "Yeah, but he's had his shots and everything. He's just ... not great with people yet."

Gage nodded. "So, I guess I should go."

Ben bit his bottom lip, looking torn. He nodded. "It was great, Gage. You were great."

Gage thought about asking for a goodbye kiss, but he was afraid Ben would say no. Instead, he pulled him into a quick hug.

He pressed a kiss to his temple. "You're pretty great, too," he said, intentionally speaking in present tense. "I hope our paths cross again."

Gage knew when he was beaten. He headed for the door before he could break down and ask again for Ben to reconsider. As he left, he heard Ben's voice, just a whisper.

"Goodbye."

Gage was bored out of his skull and sulking over Ben during office hours later that afternoon. Typically, he used the time to catch up on planning and grading, because students preferred to catch him in class with their questions.

So, when the door opened, he knew who it would be before she stepped inside. He and Chloe had an open-door policy, and they often dropped by each other's offices to have a quick chat.

"I just came by to tell you I'm glad you're alive."

He scowled at that.

"You know I don't celebrate birthdays."

That wasn't precisely true. He celebrated birthdays, just not his own. He'd grown up first with a drug addict mother, then in foster care. In the years his mother hadn't been too high to miss his birthday entirely, she'd usually opted to spend her money on meth instead of presents. Though he did remember one year she'd gotten him an ostentatious ring with a fake ruby out of a quarter machine.

He'd treasured that damn thing, wearing it until his finger turned green and all the gold paint rubbed off the cheap material. He'd worn it even though some of the boys at school had made fun of him for wearing girly jewelry.

Of course, once he was in foster care, it was hit and miss. Some of the families were really nice, and they remembered his birth date from the file or asked him about it. Others could care less, and he hadn't bothered to point it out when the day came and went without fanfare. After so much disappointment, he preferred not to focus on his birthday. Even when people wanted to do nice things, it only made him remember all the crap that came before.

"Did I say happy birthday?" Chloe said, fully aware of his aversion to the date. "I just wanted to come say hi and revel in your glorious existence."

A reluctant smile tugged at his lips. "I *am* glorious."

Not that he felt it after Ben's rejection that morning.

She settled herself in the chair across from his desk. "Why so glum? I thought you'd be in a better mood after scoring with your nurse last night."

Gage made a face. "I didn't *score* with him. I really like him. He's a good guy who deserves more respect than being treated like a piece of ass."

Chloe lifted her hands up. "Sorry, you know me. I have no tact."

Too true.

"But if you like him that much, shouldn't you be over the moon right now?"

Gage shrugged a shoulder, his face burning at the memory of Ben's rejection.

"Maybe I would be if he hadn't been in such a hurry to shut me down."

Chloe winced. "Ouch, so did you even ...?"

Gage rolled his eyes. "Yes. This was afterward."

She looked pained on his behalf. "Like immediately? Maybe you should work on your technique."

He grabbed a pen from the cup full on his desk and tossed it at her while she snickered.

"No, not immediately," he said, "but thanks for the vote of confidence."

"I'm just kidding," she said, but he could tell by her expression that she wasn't done fucking with him. "I'm sure it was ... fine."

"It was better than fine!"

"Okay ... ish."

He started fishing for another object to throw, snatching up a pencil this time. She threw up her hands and laughed. "Okay, I'm sorry. I'm sure it was mind-blowing! Don't hurt me!"

He dropped his lead-infused weapon and leaned back in his chair. "Thank you."

"Was it mind-blowing?" she asked curiously.

"You know I don't give out details."

"Come on," she whined, "I'm not asking about his blowjob technique."

"Good, because I don't know," he said with a smirk. "But yeah, it was pretty damn good. Like Pulitzer Prize-winning good."

She wrinkled her nose, and he amended his statement to something she'd appreciate.

"A Tony-winning performance."

She brightened. "Well then, that's great. We should celebrate."

"Did you miss the part where he dumped me?" Gage asked.

"Besides, you're just looking for a covert reason to celebrate my birthday, and you know I don't do that."

"Well, maybe I want to celebrate your life," she said with a pout.

It was mostly for show, so he didn't let it sway him. He did, however, soften a little at the mush.

"You do that every day by being my best friend. I don't know what I did to get on your good side, but I'm damn glad. You can be scary when you're angry."

She smirked. "Who me?"

Then she turned serious, a rare occurrence with Chloe. "Sorry it didn't work out with Ben. You two looked good together last night."

He shrugged, trying to downplay his disappointment. Chloe razzed him all the time, so when she softened, he knew he must be throwing out crybaby vibes.

"Guess I'll just have to get out more and try again, huh?"

She grinned. "Definitely. We could go tonight—"

Gage held up his hands to stop her before she steamrolled him into another bar outing. "Maybe give me a week to recover, and stop trying to get me to party on my birthday."

"I thought you didn't have a birthday," she challenged.

"You know what I mean," he groused. "And next time we go out, it has to be a gay bar."

She did a happy dance in her chair. "No birthdays, no straight bars. Time to recover. Got it."

"God help me."

6

Ben arrived a few minutes early for his shift Saturday afternoon, stopping in the locker room to drop off his belongings before heading for the nurses station and collecting his charts. Alex was waiting with a grin that made his step falter.

"What now?"

"Boyfriend," she trilled.

"Another one already?"

It had only been a week since the last motorcycle accident came through their doors, and just two days since he'd fallen into bed with Gage. His heart wrenched in his chest as he thought of the man's crestfallen expression the last time he'd seen him. He'd felt a bit cruel, throwing Gage's earnest interest back in his face, but he had to protect himself.

Alex shook her head. "Same one."

Ben's mouth dropped open. *Gage was here again?*

"You're kidding."

He grabbed the chart Alex waved around as evidence and scanned it.

"Except he's apparently not a biker today," Alex said, "and he has a tasty young guy with him. So, maybe he's not for you, after all."

Alex grabbed the chart as if to take it, but not before Ben saw that Gage had come in for X-rays on his wrist. Ben yanked back with too much force, and she let go. Stumbling a step, he scowled at her.

"You are talking nonsense."

She grinned. "Go see for yourself then. They're still in the waiting room. It's been busy."

Oh, he intended to do just that.

Gage sat in a hard plastic chair, wrist cradled by his other hand and held carefully against his stomach. Pain throbbed through it, keeping time with his heartbeat. Beside him, Zane kept up a running dialogue of his failures as a rock climber.

"I told you to stay calm, dude," Zane said, shaking his head. "You did this to yourself."

"I get it, Zane."

"But you just flailed!" Zane said, throwing his arms wide and nearly jostling Gage's arm in the process. "You panicked and slammed your own fucking hand into the rock face."

They'd been through this multiple times already. Once, while he was still in the air, tethered to a rope and cursing a blue streak. Again when he'd arrived safely to the ground and Zane had to help unharness him. That wasn't awkward or anything, having a student's hands practically in his crotch.

Then again in the car on the way over.

"Zane!" he snapped. "Watch your own flailing, and how about a little respect for your teacher."

"Sorry," Zane muttered, glancing at Gage's swelling wrist.

Damn, but he wished they'd hurry up and get him into a

room. Not for the first time, he thought he probably should have gone to an urgent care clinic instead of the ER. Not for the first time, he wondered if he'd come here in the hopes of seeing Ben again.

That would be stupid, for a number of reasons. Ben might not even be working, and even if he was, he wouldn't want to see Gage. He'd gotten what he wanted, and he'd tossed Gage out like the cold remains of a dinner that was no longer appealing.

"Hey," Zane said. "I think that pissed off nurse is headed our way."

Uh-oh. Gage's heart flipped in his chest, and he swallowed nervously. *Maybe it wouldn't be him. Maybe ...*

He looked up, and his eyes connected with Ben's across the room. Yep, it was him. And Zane wasn't kidding. Gone was the sympathetic smile and warm eyes from his last visit. Nurse Hotness looked mad as hell.

"Hey, that nurse is kind of cute, though," Zane said.

"Get your own," Gage muttered. "This one is mine."

Ben crossed the waiting room, watching Gage talk with the young guy beside him.

He was far too young for Gage, college-aged, but then some of Gage's crowd at the bar had been pretty young. Could he have already moved on to a new guy?

The kid was cute, with short dark hair and dark eyes. He was long and lanky, taller than Gage, maybe. Not a carbon copy of Ben, who had lighter hair and eyes, but definitely not out of range if Gage had a "type."

Ben felt a prickle of betrayal, and shoved the feeling down as far as it would go. This was why he had told Gage he didn't want more than a one-time hook-up. Gage talked a good game about wanting something with Ben, but he was quick to replace him.

A gorgeous man like that probably had a different guy in his bed every week. Heck, every other day.

His gaze strayed to the wrist Gage cradled, and concern washed away his brief moment of jealousy. What had Gage gone and done now? The man was careless with his safety.

Gage's new boyfriend started laughing just as he arrived.

"Dude, really?"

"Shut up," Gage gritted out, his gaze flicking up to Ben as he came to a stop before them.

Ben crossed his arms over his chest, his default defensive pose. He knew it, but he couldn't seem to break the habit.

"I thought I said I didn't want to see you around the ER again?"

He lifted an eyebrow, waiting for Gage to explain himself. Instead, the guy at his side spoke.

"Ouch! Burn," he said playfully, slapping Gage's knee. "Apparently your nurse has no problem adding insult to injury."

Gage winced. "Hello again, Ben. I'm glad to see you anyway."

He attempted a small smile, but it looked strained. Whether it was from pain caused by his wrist or the awkward situation, Ben didn't know.

"If you can't ride safely, maybe you shouldn't ride."

Before Gage could speak, the kid was at it again.

"Oh, he wasn't riding," Zane said, laughing. "You won't believe how he hurt his wrist. We were rock climbing at the indoor sports complex. You know the one?"

Ben nodded, curious now.

"Anyway, near the top he loses his grip and falls, right? No biggie because he's harnessed up and that's why I'm at the bottom, right? To make sure he doesn't crash to the ground."

"Right," Ben said. "So? What happened then?"

"Dude panics. Grabs at the rope, somehow gets his hand all twisted up, and then, while I am telling him to just be calm, that I've got him, he starts thrashing in mid-air. Smacked his own wrist against the rock wall. And I guess the way he had it twisted in that rope probably made it worse." He paused to grimace. "Painful, man. Just painful to watch."

"It wasn't exactly a great feeling either, Zane," Gage muttered. "But thanks for explaining exactly how stupid I am for Ben. I'm sure he appreciates it."

Ben couldn't fight a smile. "I did, actually. You're quite the storyteller, Zane. I can actually picture it happening."

Somehow in the telling of that story, Ben came to realize that Zane couldn't be a boyfriend. There were no vibes of attraction between them. Zane treated Gage like a buddy, and Gage seemed more annoyed by Zane than anything else.

Zane's next words seemed to confirm his suspicions.

"Yeah, I'm in his journalism class. Hoping to be telling stories as a career."

Ben knew Gage was a teacher. He'd heard enough about it at the bar that night, but he hadn't known it was college-level journalism he taught. They didn't exactly waste a lot of time on personal details like that.

"Oh, you're a student?" Ben said, turning his gaze to Gage. "I knew you were a teacher, but I didn't realize I should be calling you professor."

Ben heard the flirtatious tone of his words and inwardly cringed. Gage was probably furious at him about the way he'd shut him down after they'd hooked up, which was just as well. Ben couldn't slip and fall back into bed with him if Gage didn't want him.

When Gage answered, nothing about his voice suggested he wanted to flirt with Ben. It should have been a relief — and it was — but it stung a little.

"Just call me Gage," he said. "Professor is more for a four-year university. I just have a bachelor's degree and practical experience in journalism. I teach at the junior college."

Gage started to move, and winced in pain. Ben felt bad for ignoring his injury as long as he had.

He dropped to a crouch in front of Gage, and reached out with his hands. "May I?"

Gage's lips parted in surprise, and he darted a look at Zane. Was he worried about the student seeing him in pain? Or had he read them wrong? If he was sleeping with Zane, maybe he didn't want Ben to get so close.

Zane seemed to sense his discomfort. He got up. "I'm gonna go get a soda. You want anything?"

Gage shook his head.

Ben waited until Zane had walked away to gently take hold of Gage's wrist and feel for breaks. He wasn't technically qualified to make a diagnosis, and they'd want to do X-rays either way, but he was pretty certain it was just a sprain.

"Told you I wasn't a biker," Gage said.

Ben's eyes flicked up. "Right. You did."

"I mean, that was my first time on a bike ever. And pretty much the last, too."

"Hmm." Ben carefully returned Gage's wrist to his lap. "I suppose that's good news for drivers everywhere."

He prepared to stand, but was stopped by Gage's other hand on his right shoulder. He squeezed once, then slid his hand over Ben's neck to his hair, where his fingers curled in the strands.

Ben froze, his eyes going to Gage's.

"So, what do you say?"

Ben had to clear his throat to speak. He was at the perfect angle to appreciate Gage's sharp cheekbones and strong jaw, and the fingers curled in his hair were sending tingles down his spine.

"Say?"

"To a date?" Gage said. "Now that I'm not a biker, I'm not off-limits, right? We could try more than just a one-night stand."

Ben sighed, and grasped Gage's hand to tug it loose from his hair. Carefully, he withdrew and stood up.

"Just because you're not a biker doesn't mean you're not an adrenaline junkie," Ben said. "That's just as bad."

"I'm not—"

"Of course not," Ben said, shaking his head with a small smile. "Maybe I'll believe you when you stop hurting yourself doing stupid things."

"I can explain all that. It's not what you think."

"You don't need to explain yourself to me, Gage. Because we're just a nurse and a patient. Nothing more."

Ben glanced over his shoulder. "I'll make sure they get you in soon. I have to start my shift."

He turned and left without another word.

"So, he likes you too, then," Zane said with a smirk, soda can grasped in his left hand.

Gage cast him a skeptical look. "Was it the glare or the scolding that tipped you off?"

Zane laughed and dropped into the seat next to him. "Okay, maybe he likes me."

"Get out of here," he said with a mock scowl, and Zane grinned. "Thanks, though, for bringing me in and waiting. And putting up with my weird nurse crush, which you should definitely not know about. Pretty sure we've gone beyond the bounds of the teacher-student relationship today."

Zane nodded thoughtfully. "It's okay, Mr. Evans. You're a

spaz, but at least you have good taste. Nurse Ben was pretty darn cute."

Cute? Nurse Ben was more like sizzling hot.

"So, um, I'm going to get some extra credit out of this, right?" Zane asked after a few moments of silence.

"Yep. Definitely."

7

—————

"What the hell are you doing?"

Gage looked up from adjusting his pads, startled by the angry voice coming from the sidewalk to his right. Approaching him at a fast clip was Ben, scowl firmly in place.

Gage smiled, thrilled to see him in spite of Ben's obvious anger. It had been a full week since his visit to the ER. After X-rays, it'd turned out he just had a sprain, but if he kept going to the hospital he was going to break the bank. He was going to need to resist the urge to run to the ER. Possibly by finding another place he could run into Ben.

"Hi," he called. "I'm just about to skateboard."

"No, you're not."

"I'm sorry?"

Ben broke into a jog, reaching his side in a few seconds. When he arrived, he was breathing heavily, which brought other activities to mind.

"Are you nuts?" Ben asked once he'd sucked in a few gasps of air. "Your leg is probably mostly better, but your wrist—"

"It's fine, Ben." He flexed his wrist, ignoring the small twinge of pain as he rotated it.

Ben slapped his hand down, making him laugh in surprise.

"Your wrist is still weak. If you injure it again so soon, you'll increase your chance of a worse sprain or break. This is a bad idea."

Gage stared at Ben, at a loss. He was touched by the nurse's concern, but also a little astonished at his audacity to actually come over and start ordering him around.

"Sorry, Ben, but I have to do this for my job."

He moved to push off, and Ben grabbed his arm, holding him back. "Wait."

"Ben!" he exclaimed. "Seriously, I'm glad you care about my well-being, but you're taking the nursing role a bit too far, don't you think?"

"Why do you have to do this for your job? You're a teacher." He took a glance around. "I don't see any students."

Ben looked truly troubled over it. Gage couldn't help but enjoy Ben's concern. It meant he wasn't totally ambivalent about Gage, no matter what he said. He wondered if he might still have a shot with the guy if he played his cards right.

"I'm teaching a class on alternative journalism, and I've committed to a series of guest columns about experiencing new things in the community."

"Okay, so new doesn't necessarily mean dangerous."

Gage grinned, even knowing it would probably piss off Ben. "Yeah, but dangerous is more interesting than writing about learning to knit."

"There's no changing your mind? It has to be this?"

Gage nodded, watching Ben warily. As much as he found the nurse ridiculously attractive, he also found him intimidating. Ben had spoken strongly, more than once, of adrenaline junkies and how he couldn't date one. He didn't know how the nurse would react to Gage's insistence on skateboarding, which honestly, kids did all the time.

But he never would have guessed Ben's next reaction in a million years.

"Fine," Ben growled, and yanked the helmet from his hands.

Gage opened his mouth to object, certain Ben was going to hurl his safety equipment across the skate park, but instead he shoved the helmet down on his own head. Then he gestured impatiently for the knee and elbow pads.

"Give them."

Gage was stunned. "What ..."

Ben reached over and began undoing his padding. "I'm going for you. At least I don't have healing road rash and a weak wrist."

"It doesn't really work that ... okay!"

He caved as Ben ripped off one of his pads. He hurriedly worked to unfasten the rest of the pads and hand them over before Ben got so overzealous he ripped something or knocked Gage on his ass in the process.

"Have you ever ridden a skateboard before?" he asked tentatively.

"Not since I was 13. Have you?"

"Uh ... well, I took a lesson, sort of, at the store."

"Uh-huh," Ben said.

He bent over to adjust the knee pads, and Gage fought the urge to check out his ass. He already knew it was perfect.

"Wish me luck," Ben said with a genuine smile, and then he positioned the board, slammed his foot down and dropped into the half-pipe with a loud whoop.

"Ben!" Gage yelled, horrified.

He was certain he was going to watch the nurse crash hard, but to his amazement, Ben sped through the half-pipe, popping up on the other side.

"Just like riding a bike!" Ben called across the distance between them.

Somehow, Gage doubted that.

"I dare you to do that twice," he taunted, enjoying the grin on Ben's face.

He couldn't fathom why Ben was so averse to adrenaline junkies when he seemed to be enjoying his own buzz. But he'd work that out later.

For now, he wanted to watch Ben laugh as he owned that skateboard.

It was all going so well. Until it wasn't.

Ben dropped back into the half-pipe, but this time he tried a trick — some sort of grab — as he reached the other side.

And failed.

Gage watched, helpless, as Ben crashed to the concrete and skidded a few feet to a stop at the bottom of the half-pipe.

"Shit!" He cursed as another skater whizzed beside Ben's head, narrowly avoiding him.

Gage found his way down as quickly as he could, and dropped to his knees next to Ben, who was slowly sitting up with a groan.

"Jesus, are you okay?" he asked, helping Ben unbuckle the helmet and pull it off.

"That hurts more than I remember from the old days."

Gage clasped Ben's face and stared into his eyes, trying to evaluate how hurt he might be. This would work much better if he was the hurt one. At least Ben had the nursing experience to help him.

"I'm so sorry," he said, dropping his hands. "How bad is it?"

A laugh burst out of Ben, taking him by surprise. "I can't believe I did that."

"That makes two of us."

"That was fucking fun," he said enthusiastically, as if he'd never had fun and was amazed to discover it.

He grabbed Gage and pressed a quick, hard kiss to his lips.

It was over before Gage could react, much less respond, which was probably good since they were in public.

"Come on," Gage said, grabbing his hand and helping Ben stand. "Let's get out of here before another skater nails us."

Ben leaned against him, moving slowly, and Gage worried he'd made light of his injuries.

"Are you really okay?"

"Just a bit bruised," Ben said. He held out his arms as they cleared the ramp and stepped on the grass, where it was safer. "See? Kept all my skin, even. Better than I can say for your track record."

Gage had to give him points for that. He was seriously relieved Ben hadn't been more injured. "Please don't do that again."

"I won't if you won't," Ben said.

"What do you mean?"

"No more dangerous experiences for your columns," he said. "Make knitting interesting."

Gage laughed. "Okay, I'll do that on one condition."

Ben lifted an eyebrow, his imperious look. It was hot as hell.

"You do the rest of these experiences with me, and we call them dates."

Ben looked hesitant, some of his previous doubt creeping into his face. He wanted the happy Ben, who'd kissed him impulsively just because he wanted, not the worried guy who was certain Gage wasn't the real deal.

"I don't know. What about when they're done?" Ben asked.

"Then, we decide if we're a good match for something more. I think we will be."

And maybe by then he'll trust me, Gage thought. He was smart enough not to say it.

"If it means I keep you out of the ER, I suppose that's a sacrifice I can make," Ben said at last.

He turned away, but Gage had seen the curl to his lips.

"You're smiling! I saw you smile, Ben. You like me."

Ben handed over the helmet. "Don't push your luck."

They exchanged a smile that made Gage's heart leap. He was so caught up in looking at Ben and reveling in his second chance that the woman's voice behind them made him jump.

"Ben? Who is this?"

Ben whirled, but not before Gage saw the guilty expression cross his face. "Mom! You're done looking at cookbooks already, huh?"

His gaze flitted to the bookstore across the street, and Gage realized that must have been how Ben spotted him at the skate park.

He and his mother looked a lot alike. She had chestnut hair, though it was shot through with gray, and warm brown eyes. Her smile was kind as she looked from Ben to Gage.

"Yes, I'd wondered where you'd wandered off to," she said, poking him in the ribs. "Then I see you kissing this handsome man. You've been holding out on me."

Ben turned tomato red, his embarrassment written all over his face, but Gage could only laugh. It was apparent Ben was out to his mother, and it wasn't likely he'd kiss Gage in public – even impulsively – if he was worried about people knowing about his sexuality.

He held out a hand to Ben's mother. "I'm Gage Evans. I met your son in the ER."

She shook his hand, smiling. "Nice to meet you, Gage. I'm Suzy Griggs. Now, tell me. Are you two dating? Because I keep offering to set him up with my friend's nephews and grandsons, but he always says no."

Gage's eyebrow quirked. *Interesting.*

Ben regularly turned down dates, and not only from him. He knew Ben had some sort of bad experience making him wary of dating, but it had been hard not to take it personally when he was being kicked out of Ben's bed after putting himself out there.

He resolved then and there not to give up on Ben. He'd win him over, even if he had to put in long, grueling hours to do it.

"Mom!" Ben protested, turning even redder. Gage had never seen someone look so embarrassed. "We're not—"

"Yes," Gage interrupted, "we're dating."

Ben turned wide eyes on him, and he couldn't suppress his own smile. "You did just agree to go on a series of dates with me. Right, Ben?"

Ben's expression faltered, as he looked between Gage and his mother, as if uncertain who was ally and who was enemy.

After a moment he rolled his eyes. "Yeah, Mom. We're dating."

While his mother squealed and hugged him, his eyes shot daggers at Gage over her shoulder. But Gage couldn't muster up even the tiniest bit of remorse. He smiled brightly at Ben until his eyes softened and his own lips twitched in a rueful smile.

Gage felt more certain than ever he could win Ben's heart. He just had to woo him a bit first.

8

"*C*ooking?"

Someone in Gage's class sounded incredulous at the idea he'd write his next column about learning to cook through a community class.

"Lame!" someone else called, and encouraged, the rest of the class started booing and razzing him.

Gage waved them off. "Yeah, yeah. You're all just disappointed I'm not falling out of the sky. My death won't save you from your assignments."

They laughed, just as he'd predicted they would.

Gage finished outlining the first article they'd be writing. They were starting with the assignment to engage in a student activity on campus they'd never experienced before. They then had to write a first-person account of that experience for the college newspaper, much like Gage was doing each week for The Ashe Sentinel.

After class, Gage gathered up his belongings as the students made their way through the door. He always waited until they were all gone before leaving, just in case someone wanted a word alone.

Today, it appeared Zane wanted a word, which was helpful. Because Gage had been meaning to talk to him about his performance in class.

"You got with that cute nurse, huh?" he asked, pausing by Gage's desk with a smirk.

Gage shrugged on his jacket and slung his leather satchel over his shoulder.

"What makes you say that?"

Zane shrugged, tucking his hands in his pockets. "Nurse didn't like seeing you hurt. Suddenly you're doing a cooking class? I can add two and two."

Gage narrowed his eyes. "This isn't a math class."

Zane laughed. "Yeah, man. I get it. None of my business."

"I think you have more important things to worry about, don't you?" Gage asked, watching Zane as he tensed up and his face closed off.

"I don't know what you mean," he mumbled.

"You've missed three classes in two weeks, and you were late today," Gage pointed out.

Anger flared in Zane's eyes. "I've turned in all my work, and you still owe me extra credit for hauling you to the ER."

Gage sat on the corner of his desk, doing his best to look calm and relaxed. He didn't speak for a moment, allowing Zane time to get hold of his emotions. He didn't know what exactly was going on with the kid, but his anger seemed out of proportion with their discussion.

"Your work hasn't been up to its usual standards," he said carefully.

Glancing at the time, he debated moving the discussion to his office, but he worried Zane would use it as an excuse to avoid finishing their talk.

Zane scoffed. "My work is 10 times better than anyone else's in the class, and you know it."

Okay, 10 times was a bit of an exaggeration. Zane was smart, and he had a natural talent for writing. He obviously knew it. Trouble was, that meant he could skate by on little to no effort and most instructors wouldn't call him on it.

"I meant it hasn't been up to your usual standard," Gage clarified. "This isn't the first class you've taken with me. I know your potential, Zane, and you're not meeting it right now."

Zane rolled his eyes. "Jesus Christ. I'm sorry I brought up the nurse, okay? I thought we were friends. Can I go now?"

Gage put a hand on Zane's arm as he started to turn away. Zane tensed, but he didn't pull away.

"We are friends," Gage said evenly, though he wouldn't ordinarily like to describe his relationship with a student that way. He sensed Zane needed a friend right now. "I'm not bringing this up to be a hardass or because you mentioned Ben. I'm a little worried about you."

Zane took a step back, shrugging off Gage's hand.

"I'm fine," he muttered, eyes on the floor.

"You know when my office hours are?" Gage asked.

Zane looked up, long dark lashes only making his dark brown eyes stand out that much more against his pale face. He really was a gorgeous guy, but Gage shut down the part of himself tempted to make a fuller appraisal of Zane's looks. He was fully invested in Ben, even if Ben was hedging his bets, and beyond that, he was Zane's teacher.

"Yeah, so?" Zane said.

Gage shrugged and stood up from his desk, preparing to leave.

"If you need to talk, you know when and where to find me. I can tell something's bothering you."

Zane looked uncomfortable. "Tell you, like ... as my teacher, you mean?"

"Or just a friend," Gage said, sensing this was paramount.

88

For whatever reason, Zane didn't want a teacher who was invested in his grades. He wanted someone who cared. Gage could do that for him.

Zane nodded stiffly. "Okay."

Hoping to see another smile, Gage tried to lighten the moment.

"You were right about the nurse," he admitted. "He didn't like me doing dangerous things. He even did the skateboarding for me."

Zane's eyes widened. "No shit? Did you fictionalize your article?" he asked as they walked out the door together.

Gage paused to close and lock the classroom door, before heading down the hall with Zane at his side.

"Nope. I told you that alternative journalism isn't lying. I just wrote the article from a slightly different perspective."

"What kind of perspective?"

"I wrote about the skate park, the experience of being there and watching the skaters. I didn't specifically say I was on a skateboard, crashing and burning. I just imagined what it might be like."

Zane laughed. "So, did Ben really crash and burn?"

"Yup," Gage said. "I felt bad, but he was pretty insistent about doing it in my place. And afterwards, he asked me not to do dangerous things anymore."

"And you gave in, you sucker," Zane taunted.

Gage chuckled. "Only because I could use it to convince him to date me. He's doing the rest of the column experiences with me."

Zane grinned and held out his fist for a bump. "Nice!"

Gage bumped his knuckles, feeling a little silly to be oversharing with his student but relieved to see the smile brightening his face.

"So, you know where to find me if you want to talk," Gage said, as they parted ways in front of the building.

Zane's smile dimmed, but it didn't fade entirely. He nodded. "Yeah, thanks man. Just some personal stuff. Hopefully, it'll be resolved soon, but ... I don't know."

He looked lost, and Gage reached out and squeezed his shoulder. "I mean it. You can talk to me, even if it has nothing to do with school."

Zane seemed to shake his mood off. "Yeah, well have fun *cooking,* you sap."

"I'll have you know that cooking is pretty darn far out of my comfort zone. Maybe further than skateboarding, so it fits the theme of the column series. Shaking it up is not a bad thing."

"Especially when it makes a cute nurse happy."

Gage laughed. "Get out of here before I dock your grade."

Zane adjusted the strap on his backpack. "Have fun tonight, Mr. Evans. Don't do anything I wouldn't do," he said, and waggled his brows.

Gage had the suspicion there wasn't much Zane wouldn't do, but he shook it off. He was wooing his man, not taking him to bed.

He grinned to himself as he headed to the student union for lunch with Chloe. In approximately six hours, he'd see Ben.

For a date.

About damn time.

Gage stood alone at his station in the couples cooking class. He felt the empty space beside him like a tangible thing. The left side of his body vibrated with tension, physically aware of the missing body heat that should be present.

He'd chosen the cooking class for Ben. Nurse Hotness

wanted him to tone down his column topics, and he wanted Ben to date him, so it was a no-brainer.

Except now it looked like Ben was going to stand him up.

Gage cursed himself again for not pushing to pick Ben up. He knew the man was skittish about dating, and he'd suspected Ben had wanted to meet him here to make their outing seem less date-like. But maybe he'd just wanted to avoid Gage, period.

The cooking teacher made the rounds, checking each station for ingredients and making sure they understood the prep instructions written out on a sheet. Gage took the opportunity to talk to the other couples, getting names and back stories about why they'd decided to try out the culinary course so he could work it into his column.

Jay and Kay — as sickeningly cute as their rhyming names — were in their early twenties and recently married.

"My mom had a full-time career, and we lived mostly on take-out," Kay said. "She didn't have the time or the skills to teach us anything about cooking, so I'm hopeless!"

"And my parents were too traditional to do something crazy like teach their son to cook," Jay said with a good-natured grin. "My mom makes the most amazing country dinners. Country-fried steak, mashed potatoes, apple pie. God, I miss it so much. I tell you, if I had any doubts about getting married ..."

Kay shoved an elbow in his gut, and he groaned theatrically, but they were both laughing.

"What about you?" Kay asked.

"Eh, I'm a burgers on the grill kind of guy. I won't starve, but I've definitely never made—" he checked the recipe sheet on the table — "Mediterranean chicken and roasted vegetables."

They made small talk about how delicious it sounded before he moved on to a middle-aged woman named Sherry. She appeared to be alone.

"I didn't realize it was couples," she said, rolling her eyes. "It was right there on the sign-up sheet, but I guess I was more interested in all the ingredients. I'm recently divorced, and my husband was really the chef in our home. I'm tired of spaghetti."

She laughed, but he could hear the underlying note of unhappiness, and he felt bad for her. It was amazing how open some people were about their lives, especially if you greet them with a smile and then listen quietly as they speak, instead of trying to inject your own opinions. He made a mental note to mention that to his students.

"I feel a little foolish, here all alone," she said.

He patted her arm. "Everyone here is focused on their own situation. No one is going to be staring at you because you're here alone."

She smiled gratefully. "You're right." She glanced back toward his table. "Are you alone too?"

He shrugged, trying to hide his feelings about Ben being a no-show. "Could be. My partner in crime isn't here yet. Cross your fingers for me."

"I will," she promised.

"If he doesn't show, we can partner up."

Her smile got brighter, and he said his goodbyes before she could ask for his number. He wanted to be friendly, not lead her on.

Ellen Mayes, owner of the culinary store hosting the lessons, began giving them instructions. The chicken thighs were already marinated in the large, industrial refrigerator. Their recipe sheet included how to perform that step on their own, but for the sake of the short class time, some prep work had been done for them.

Gage followed orders, grabbing his servings of chicken and unloading the basket at his cooking station of all the produce that would be included in the meal. Onion, bell pepper, potatoes and zucchini lined the counter when he was done.

Ellen explained that ideally they would have marinated the vegetables overnight, but tonight they were just going to baste them in the marinade.

"Kind of pointless to have a cooking class if I do all the prep work. So, get started on cutting those vegetables. I'll come around and offer some tips on your knife work as you do it. If you're good with a knife, cooking becomes so much easier and faster. You won't believe how much it can change your life."

Gage grabbed the zucchini, prepared to get started.

"Your partner couldn't make it?" Ellen asked, coming to a stop by his station. They'd already spoken earlier, and she was aware he was writing a column about the class.

Gage started to nod when movement at the door caught his eye.

Ben.

A relieved breath gushed out of his chest, and he couldn't hold back a big grin. "There he is now."

Ben rushed over, still dressed in scrubs. He was getting more than one curious look from the rest of the room.

"I am so sorry," Ben said, laying a hand on Gage's arm. His brown eyes were so warm Gage felt all his irritation evaporate. "It was my day off, but I got called in to cover a shift, and then there was a trauma and I had to stay late. I didn't even have time to go home."

Gage's eyebrow hitched as he took in the drab scrubs. "Obviously."

Ben waved a hand. "I showered and put on clean scrubs at the hospital—"

"Are you a doctor?" Kay asked, while some of the other couples glanced over curiously.

Ben tossed a distracted glance her way. "Nurse, actually."

"Oh, that's great," she said, but it sounded like a throwaway line designed to end the conversation before turning back to her own station.

"Does that bother you?" Gage asked in a low voice.

Ben looked confused. "What?"

He nodded his head toward Kay, who was now studiously chopping vegetables. "People asking if you're a doctor, and ..."

He trailed off, not certain he should voice his observation. He didn't want to be shot for being the messenger.

Ben snorted. "Then suddenly uninterested when they find out I'm a nurse? Yeah, I get that plenty. Probably more than the female nurses. Sexism at its finest. People assume they're nurses, even if they're doctors, and they assume I must be a doctor or paramedic because I'm a man, because nursing couldn't possibly be a good enough career for me. It's annoying, but what can you do?"

Gage knew very little about Ben's profession, but he did know that Ben was an excellent nurse who'd made him far more comfortable than the doctors, and not just because he was cute. Ben had a nurturing warmth to him that probably meant the world to a lot of patients and family members.

"Well, I think you're a great nurse," he said. "And you were way more important to me in the ER than that sadist Dr. Johnston."

Ben laughed. "You're just saying that because he stuck a needle in you."

"Busted."

"I've done my fair share of pricking men, too."

"Are you flirting with me, nurse?"

Ben rolled his eyes, but his smile gave him away. He was being a total flirt, and Gage loved every second of it.

"I'm sorry again for being so late," Ben said.

Gage nudged him playfully. "I thought you stood me up."

Ben looked horrified at the notion, even with their rocky

beginning and strange dating arrangement. "I would never do that!"

Gage laughed. "It's okay. I'm glad you're here. It's nice to see you again."

Ben, for once, appeared to let his guard down.

"Yeah, you too." He turned to the counter and surveyed the veggies. "So, what now?"

"Listen up, everybody," Ellen called from the front. "You have 15 minutes to finish your prep. Then we'll move on from there."

"You heard the lady," Gage teased. "Get chopping."

"Ha," Ben said, handing Gage one of the knives. "You do the onions, since this is for your column. I'll do the zucchini."

They both set to chopping their ingredients. Ben was pretty decent with a knife. After their little talk, Gage didn't want to ask Ben why he hadn't become a doctor, but he was curious.

Maybe Ben didn't have the stomach for surgery. Then again, he *was* a trauma nurse. Maybe he just liked working with people. Most doctors had a crappy bedside manner, while Ben was effortlessly friendly.

"You ever seen anything really gory at work? Like blood shooting out in a spray—"

Ben jerked toward Gage, brandishing his knife perilously close to Gage's face.

"You really think that's a great subject while prepping food?"

"Whoa," Gage said, edging away a bit. "Put that thing away. I chose this cooking class just for you, thinking it would be less dangerous."

"Very funny," Ben said, bumping Gage's shoulder playfully just as he picked up his knife once more.

His grip was loose and the knife tumbled from his fingers. It fell directly toward the floor — and his feet.

In retrospect, wearing flip-flops might have been a bad

choice. The tip of the knife skated over one strap, nicked the top of his foot and flipped over onto the floor with a clatter.

"Crap!" he hissed.

Ben clapped a hand over his mouth, his eyes rounding in horror. "Oh my god, Gage!"

Then, before Gage could reassure him it wasn't serious, he dropped to the ground at his feet and examined the minuscule cut on his foot. It was bleeding, but it was the size of a paper cut. The knife had barely scratched him.

Ben looked up apologetically. "I'm a klutz. I don't know if you knew that."

"Must be awkward in the ER."

"If you can make fun of me, I think you'll live," he said dryly. He took a second look at Gage's foot. "You should think about trimming those toenails."

Everyone in the class was watching them with concern. Well, some concern and some horrified fascination, much as you'd see at the scene of a train wreck, literal or figurative.

Seeing Ben kneeling at his feet wasn't doing his imagination any favors, either. He figured he'd better put an end to this tableau before the other couples saw something they shouldn't.

Gage grabbed Ben's arms, hauling him to his feet. "Okay, nurse. Thank you for that diagnosis."

Ben smirked. "Would you like me to get the first aid kit from my car?"

Ellen came up beside their station. "We have one in the store. Let me grab you a Band-Aid and some disinfectant. Make sure you get a clean knife and both of you wash your hands before you resume."

"Thanks," Gage said.

Ben looked slightly abashed. "Sorry," he muttered.

"You *should* apologize. I thought you didn't want me injured again," Gage said, rubbing it in.

When Ben scowled, he laughed and leaned in to whisper in his ear. "I really think you owe me a kiss to make up for that. You made me bleed."

Ben gave him the evil eye, but a smile pulled at his lips. "We'll see."

Good enough. Inside, Gage punched the air and cheered. On the outside, he tried to play it casual.

"Come on, nurse. Fix me up, so we can get back to work on this Mediterranean chicken dish."

The rest of evening went smoothly, and they managed to chop all their veggies without any more injuries. The rest of the recipe had been fairly simple. They poured extra marinade over the vegetables, dumped it all in a foil-lined pan and stuck it in the oven. While it cooked, Ellen gave them wine and demonstrated how to make a no-bake cheesecake, before stashing it in the freezer.

"It needs to freeze overnight," she said, to a room full of disappointed groans.

Smiling, she reached into the freezer and removed a cake ready to serve. "Which is why I prepared one last night, so we could eat it."

That was met with much excitement, and they all crowded around to grab plates and slices of cake to eat while the main dish baked in the oven.

"I like the way you think," Gage teased her, "dessert before dinner."

She laughed. "A little backwards, maybe."

"It's delicious," Ben volunteered, his eyes closing in pleasure as he took another bite. Gage watched him eat his cake, unable to take his eyes off Ben's mouth.

When he was nearly done, Ben glanced up at him and froze in the act of licking a crumb from the corner of his mouth.

Gage reached out, catching it on his thumb. He intended to

wipe it away, even though he desperately wanted to lick it off Ben. Before he could draw away, Ben turned his head and sucked his thumb into his mouth. His tongue swirled around, causing all kinds of interesting things to happen in Gage's pants, before pulling back.

"It's all mine. You can't have it," he said teasingly, but Gage saw the heat in his eyes. Ben still wanted him, even if he was hesitant to leap back into anything.

Gage shifted behind the counter, where he could adjust himself.

"Now you definitely owe me a kiss," he muttered.

"Just don't get your hopes up that kiss is going anywhere but your lips," Ben warned.

Man, did that give him some ideas. He shifted again, glaring at Ben, the little tease, but he couldn't hold in a big smile.

He'd suffer any amount of teasing for the chance to kiss Ben.

Ben was nervous when they walked out with the rest of their class, everyone heading for their cars. As much as they'd joked about Ben owing Gage a kiss, he could hardly do it in public, and there was no way he was taking Gage home. He'd never *stop* with one kiss.

"Well, guess this is goodnight," he said.

"Yep. It was fun."

"It was," Ben agreed wholeheartedly.

The more time he spent with Gage, the more he liked him. Which was why he needed to proceed with caution. He'd agreed to do these so-called dates with Gage, but it didn't have to be anything more than a couple of friends hanging out. He could use a friend outside of the hospital anyway. His mom was pretty much his only contact outside the ER these days.

Ben shifted toward the parking lot. "Well, guess I better be going. Just text me with the details for next week."

Gage put a hand on his wrist. "Hold up. Aren't you forgetting something?"

Ben's heart sped up. "Um, but there's people around, so ..."

Gage grinned. "Trust me," he said, and then he was pulling Ben by the hand down the sidewalk.

"Gage, maybe you haven't figured this out, but I'm not so great with the trust thing," he said. "Please tell me where we're going."

Gage turned into a side lot of the store, out of sight of the rest of the cooking class attendees. He pulled Ben around the corner after him, and pressed him against the rough brick exterior.

It was dark on this side of the store, so dark Ben couldn't see Gage's eye color, but he could make out enough of his expression to see a smile.

"Just right here," he murmured.

The trickle of unease he'd felt slid away. This was Gage. He was larger and stronger than Ben, but he hadn't been aggressive at all the night they hooked up. Even the way he'd pressed Ben up against the bricks had been gentle.

Gage leaned in and whispered in his ear. "Can I kiss you?"

Just hearing him ask permission had Ben melting on the spot. He nodded jerkily, unable to find his voice as Gage's breath heated his neck.

Slowly, Gage pulled back and cradled Ben's face in his hands.

Ben was burning for that kiss, so worked up the blood rushed loudly in his ears. His dick was getting hard, and Gage's lips hadn't even met his yet.

Just a kiss, he reminded himself. *No sex.*

Gage leaned in and brushed a kiss across his lips.

Ben's lips parted, a sigh slipping free, as he relaxed under Gage's touch. To his shock, Gage didn't take the invitation to deepen the kiss. Dry lips brushed together briefly before air swept in between them.

Ben's eyes shot open. "What was that?"

Gage grinned. "It was a kiss. I'm being a gentleman here," he said. "Someone once told me it was better to leave them wanting more, so ..."

"Fuck that," Ben growled.

Gage's laugh of surprise was cut off abruptly as Ben grabbed a fistful of his shirt and yanked him in for a real kiss.

Ben caught Gage's lips with his, and swallowed down the last of his muffled laugh. Soon enough, the laughter turned to a moan as their tongues touched.

Gage's hands dropped to Ben's waist and pulled them tighter together. He was just as hard in his jeans as Ben was.

Ben instinctively rolled his hips against Gage before he remembered this was just a kiss.

He tore himself away, pushing his hands against Gage's chest to create some breathing room. Gage gasped for air, staring at him with burning eyes.

Ben was certain he was about to curse him as a cock tease, and he wouldn't be able to deny it. He'd teased his own damn cock mercilessly. It throbbed in complaint in his jeans.

"This doesn't have to be goodnight," Gage said.

Ben bit his lip, fighting to resist the little voice in his head. *One more time*, it whispered, *one more time won't hurt.*

"Forget I said that," Gage said before Ben could wrestle out a decision. "You need time to trust I'm not just a flash in the pan."

Ben quirked a brow, not entirely certain what he meant by that.

"That I'm serious about you," Gage clarified.

Ben took a deep breath and nodded. "Right. I'm a little skittish about relationships right now."

"So, you finally admit it's not the whole biker thing?" Gage said as they began walking back toward the parking lot.

"It doesn't help," Ben said. "My last two ... whatever they were weren't the type to settle down. Tripp was a biker, and we were just casual, as much as I wanted it to be otherwise, and my college boyfriend was a serious adrenaline junkie. He was a big-time mountain climber. He actually hated Kansas," Ben said with a laugh. "He did the indoor climbing walls and took weekend trips to Colorado whenever he could."

This was the most open Ben had been about his reluctance to date. Gage kept quiet a moment longer to make sure Ben didn't have anything else to share. If he spoke up, Ben would probably clam up again.

"Geez, I'm rambling. See what you did to my brain cells," Ben said with a light laugh.

"Talk as much as you want. I like learning more about you," Gage said.

They came to a stop next to Ben's car, one of only two in the lot at this point. Ben fidgeted with his keys nervously.

"You've only had two boyfriends?" Gage asked, now that he was certain Ben was done volunteering information.

Ben laughed. "Not even two. Tripp was casual, like I said. There have been other guys, but no one serious enough to be called a boyfriend. I'm far from virginal, though."

Gage grinned. "I know, believe me."

"What about you? If I get the third degree, so do you."

His smile faded. It was more fun to grill Ben than open up himself, but turnabout was fair play.

"I spent a few years doing the club scene. I used to live in Kansas City, so I had more options. But like I told Chloe, it's pretty tough to find love over a bathroom blowjob."

"You said that to Chloe?" Ben said with a surprised laugh.

"We pretty much tell each other everything," he said. "We'd be married by now if she was a man."

Ben cocked his head. "So, you've never been in love?"

Gage could sense the shutdown coming. If Ben didn't believe he was capable of love, he'd be even more skittish. And besides, he could love. He *had* loved.

"I have been," he said reluctantly. "It was in high school, and he was in the closet."

"Ouch."

"Yeah," Gage said. "I was kind of considered a bad boy back then. Long story. Mainly it wasn't true, but I came from the wrong side of the tracks. He was super smart and got into an Ivy League school. There was no way I could follow him."

"You didn't try long-distance?"

"Nah, Nate was way too paranoid about getting outed. He wouldn't ever email me or text me. So forget about video chat."

"That sounds shitty."

Gage hated the sound of pity in Ben's voice. He was over this. It was over a long time ago, and he was so damn young. They never would have lasted.

"Yep. Besides, I ran into him a few years ago. He got married."

"To a woman?"

"Yep. We didn't talk much because his wife was there and we were on a public sidewalk, but he made a comment about going through crazy phases in high school, and I got the hint."

"Jesus, Gage, maybe *you* should be skittish about dating."

Gage laughed, and squeezed Ben's hand. They'd been talking for 10 minutes in an empty parking lot. Probably time to call it a night.

"Maybe I have been," he said.

Truth be told, though, he just dealt with his fears differently than Ben did. While Ben ran away, trying to maintain distance,

Gage tried to latch on, desperate for an anchor. It was difficult not having a family to call his own. If it wasn't for Chloe, he'd be totally adrift, but they'd become super close friends in college. She was the reason he'd gotten a job in Ashe in the first place.

Gage knew what he was doing, knew he had abandonment issues that caused him to cling to people, but he couldn't seem to break the habit. He was scared to death he'd ruin everything with Ben, but at least with Ben pulling away so often, Gage didn't have much chance to suffocate him.

Way to find the silver lining, Gage.

"It was a long time ago, though," Gage said, brushing off the memory of his high school boyfriend. "And I'm not really into the bar hook-up thing."

Ben winced, a guilty expression on his face.

Gage leaned in and kissed his cheek. "Don't feel bad. You weren't a bar hook-up to me, and whatever happens, I know you didn't make me any promises about having a relationship. I just hoped."

"I know what it's like to hope," Ben said softly.

They whispered goodnight, exchanged one more chaste kiss similar to the one Gage had teased Ben with earlier, and went their separate ways. Despite having to air some of his less pleasant relationship history, Gage smiled all the way to the car.

He felt like he'd had a real breakthrough with Ben. If he was patient, he could earn his trust and get everything he wanted with the man.

He really believed that.

9

Ben hesitated at the edge of the skating rink with trepidation. It had been a lot of years since he'd been skating, and his very brief interlude with skateboarding had proven it was *not* like riding a bike. Then again, he hadn't ridden a bicycle in long enough, maybe it was, and that saying was a complete fallacy.

"Why skating?" he asked. "Why is everything about the wheels with you?"

"I thought we should give the knives a rest," Gage deadpanned.

He stepped onto the rink with only a slight wobble of unsteadiness. "It was nostalgia, I suppose," he said, giving Ben a serious answer. "I thought it'd be fun. Besides, young children go roller skating, so you can't possibly call me reckless."

Ben followed him onto the rink, and his feet flew from under him. He grabbed Gage's arms frantically, like a man drowning, and crashed against his chest while he tried to get his feet back under him where they belonged. Gage laughed while he helped pull him up.

Close to Ben's ear, he said, "I didn't expect the added benefit of you falling all over me. How were you so good on a skate-board and so bad at this?"

Finally, Ben was able to stand on his own.

"Asshole," he muttered, before slowly drawing back into his own space. He cast a glance around to see if anyone had noticed their closeness in a way that spelled trouble.

"As you may recall, I crashed and burned on that skateboard. Besides, it's completely different than having my feet slipping and sliding under me."

"Come on," Gage called, already several feet away, gliding effortlessly over the floor.

At last, his tendency to harm himself on these excursions seemed to disappear. Unfortunately, Ben seemed like the next likely candidate for injury. He skated awkwardly, clinging to the walls and flailing every few seconds in an attempt to stay on his feet.

Gage slowed down and dropped back to stay by his side. Ben gave up his worries that someone might take their closeness the wrong way and clung to Gage's arm. Anyone could see he was barely staying on his feet, so he wasn't too worried about homophobia rearing its ugly head.

"So, tell me more about yourself," Gage said. "Any brothers or sisters?"

Ben was mostly focused on his balance, so he answered on autopilot.

"I was a miracle baby," Ben said with a smile. "Maybe that's why ..."

He trailed off, the smile sliding away with his words. He'd nearly spoken his thought out loud.

He was a miracle to his parents. Maybe that's why it bothered him so much he'd been unable to find love. To be cherished like that, treated as a precious gift by his parents his whole childhood and then to be so easily discarded by men. ...

He'd been so surprised, so devastated to learn he wasn't special.

"Why what?" Gage prompted.

Ben shook his head. "Nothing. Maybe that's why I'm so close with my mother."

Gage mock gasped. "Oh no, a Mama's boy?"

Ben laughed and slugged his shoulder. "Shut up."

Gage's eyes gleamed with amusement, then with heat. "Careful, or you'll have to nurse my injuries. Not that I'm complaining. Somehow you make even those hideous scrubs look good."

Ben's face heated with a blush, and he turned his head away to hide his expression. It wouldn't do to get too close. He'd learned that lesson too many times to fall again.

With his heart, not his body, anyway. His body proceeded to fall the moment he turned too quickly.

Gage made a grab for Ben when he lost his balance, but he was too slow. He'd been enthralled by the blush on Ben's cheeks, wondering if he might have a chance at another steamy kiss like the one they'd shared a week ago. Or more.

Ben sprawled at his feet, and Gage nearly tripped over him. He turned his feet in his skates, circling back around so he was in front of Ben.

"You okay?"

He reached down to grab Ben's hand and help lever him up, but it ended up being more of a full body experience as Ben struggled on the skates. He grabbed onto Gage's shoulders and clung to him.

"Ow, shit, my ass hurts."

Gage chuckled breathlessly, back aching from trying to keep

them both from falling back down in a heap. "I can think of some much better ways to make your ass hurt."

"You and me both," Ben muttered.

Damn. Gage's hands clenched on Ben's waist. He wasn't going to get a better opening than that.

"I've gotten enough of the skating experience. How about we take this somewhere else. Like your place?"

He couldn't say that Ben tensed in his arms, because Ben was already incredibly tense. But he did push away, clunking over the floor in steps, rather than rolling glides, until he got to a wall. He found the nearest exit from the rink and took it.

Was that a yes?

Gage followed, his heart beating fast.

Once on carpet, they were more equal again. Gage watched Ben's face, seeing the struggle there. Hoping to tilt it in his favor, he added: "I'd never hurt you, you know. I'm fairly certain, if anything, you'll end up hurting me."

Ben looked surprised at that thought. That he could break Gage's heart. "Why would you want to take that risk?"

"Because you're worth it. Because I am." He shrugged a shoulder. "Better to have loved and lost than never ..."

Ben rolled his eyes. "Okay, Shakespeare."

"Actually, it was Tennyson—"

"A know-it-all, too. I really know how to pick them."

Gage grinned, hope flaring in his chest. "Have you picked me, then?"

Ben shook his head, but a smile tugged at his lips. "Get me out of these awful skates, and then we'll see."

"Yessss!" Gage threw his fist in the air in victory. "And the crowd goes wild."

He would have preferred to kiss Ben in celebration, but it wasn't something he could do in the crowded skating rink.

Instead, he settled for thinking about all the things he might finally get to repeat with Ben once they left.

Ben was quiet on the way back to his house, and Gage was almost certain he was going to change his mind. But when he pulled into the drive, Ben glanced over with a mischievous smile.

"Coming in?"

"Hell, yes!"

Ben laughed at his enthusiasm, eyes bright. Gone was the distant, tense man who'd kicked Gage out of his bedroom the morning after they'd first hooked up.

"Come on, then."

Gage followed him inside. His blood thrummed with anticipation, and he was almost more anxious than the first time they slept together. It had been fantastic before, but that also meant there were high expectations.

Ben headed for the kitchen, so Gage trailed after him like the lovesick puppy he was.

"Bruiser! Here kitty!"

He grabbed a bag of cat food from the pantry and began pouring a bowl. From the back of the house, Gage heard a quiet meow and the thump of a cat jumping to the floor.

"He's not going to attack my feet again, is he?"

Ben cast a look over his shoulder, a smile tugging at the corners of his mouth. "There are no guarantees. But you like to live dangerously, right?"

"No," Gage countered, circling the kitchen island to snag Ben around the waist and pull him flush against his body. "You just tell yourself that so you don't have to give me a chance."

Ben pulled away. "Are we going to do this now?"

Gage cocked his head, watching Ben move so that the breakfast bar was situated between them once again. It didn't stop Gage from noticing the rigid set to Ben's shoulders or the flush in his cheeks that was sadly not from arousal.

"We can do anything you want," he said carefully.

Ben relaxed a fraction. "You mean that, don't you?"

Grabbing an orange from the bowl of fruit on the counter, he tossed it from one hand to the other, giving away his nerves.

"You're not angry about what happened last time you were here?"

Gage shrugged a shoulder. "A little at first, but mostly I was disappointed."

Bruiser finally slunk into the kitchen behind Ben, ignoring Gage completely to his relief, and sniffed around his bowl. He looked down at the food as if he was far too good to eat it — though maybe that was just the impression his squashed face gave — before turning to give Ben a plaintive meow.

Ben dropped to a crouch and stroked his hand down Bruiser's body, starting at his head and running down this spine to the very tip of his tail. Bruiser arched into his touch, looking far more tame than the last time Gage saw him.

"I'm sorry," Ben said finally, without looking up from Bruiser. "I'm amazed you even talked to me after that."

"Don't get me wrong. I'd rather it didn't happen again."

Ben stood, turning to face him. Bruiser sneezed loudly behind him and tucked into his dinner.

"So, what are we doing, Gage? Dating?"

"Technically, we're already dating," he pointed out. "I asked you to consider these outings dates. To see where things might go."

"True, but ..."

Ben trailed off, nibbling on his bottom lip. Gage had already noticed he did that whenever he was nervous.

Gage didn't want to have this talk with a barrier between them. He edged between Bruiser's swishing tail and the counter so he could take Ben's hands in his own. Lifting them, he kissed the back of each one.

"What do you want, Ben?"

Ben looked up, brown eyes intent. His voice was hardly more than a whisper when he admitted the truth. "I want you."

Gage dropped his head to kiss him, and Ben slid his arms around his neck.

"Whatever you want," Gage murmured against Ben's cheek.

"Can we just not do the whole define the relationship thing. Just see where it goes?"

It wasn't everything Gage wanted, but it was a hell of a lot more than he expected to get when they began the drive to Ben's place. He could be patient. Eventually, Ben would give in. He had too much heart to do anything else.

"Anything you want," he repeated, before kissing him again.

Ben led Gage to the bedroom, where they slowly undressed each other. Unlike the first time they'd been together, when he was amped with lust and eager to fuck hard, Ben didn't feel the urge to hurry. They shared lingering kisses in between removing shirts and jeans and socks and shoes.

When he was down to his boxer briefs, he slipped into the bed and Gage followed. They moved into each other's arms, kissing and rubbing together. Taking their time.

Gage kissed his body so softly, so gently, Ben's chest grew tight with emotion. They still had so much to learn about each other, but this was more intimacy than he'd ever had with Tripp. He'd always treated Ben like a means to an end. Gage treated him like the journey was just as important as the destination.

The urge to pull away and create more distance was there, but Ben fought it. Just once, he wanted to experience this feeling of being another man's treasure. Even if it was temporary. Even if it was so fragile it shattered later. He'd have this memory, this knowledge that it could happen.

So, when Gage started whispering sweet words, Ben didn't roll away and change positions to distract him as he'd done before. He closed his eyes, unable to look into Gage's intense blue gaze, but let those soft words of praise soak into him. He let them resonate within him as warmth spread through his limbs.

You're sexy.

You're amazing.

You're everything I could want.

By the time Gage pushed inside him, after kissing and licking what seemed like every inch of his body, Ben was trembling with need, and emotion threatened to break him apart.

He wrapped his arms and legs around Gage and held on tight, riding out the waves of pleasure. It was unlike him to be so passive — he didn't always top from the bottom, but he pretty much always gave as much as he received.

Not this time.

He didn't even take care of his own pleasure. Gage wrapped a hand around him at just the right moment, stroking him in time with his thrusts, and Ben came with a shuddering moan. Gage managed three more thrusts before he came, as well.

When he pulled out and dropped to the side, Ben's insecurities kicked in.

"I'm sorry," he mumbled.

"Why are you sorry?" Gage asked, the wrinkle in his brow giving away his confusion. "That was really good. For me, anyway. Was it not good for you?"

Jesus, now he was giving Gage a complex. The man deserved nothing but praise.

"No, it was great," Ben reassured him. "It's just, I'm not usually so. ..."

"So what?"

"Selfish," Ben blurted, his cheeks flaming. "I just let you do all the work." He threw an arm over his eyes, unable to look at Gage. "God, I was a cold fish, wasn't I? I'm sorry."

Gage pulled down his arm, but Ben kept his eyes squeezed shut.

"Ben, are you nuts?"

Gage's incredulous tone had his eyes popping open despite his mortification. Ben looked uncertainly into Gage's light blue gaze, fixed on him so intently his skin prickled.

"You don't have to take charge for it to be good. I realize you're a bit of a control freak about sex—"

"No, I'm not!"

Gage laughed. "I'm just saying that today was amazing because I got to watch you just let go and unravel under me. That's just as exciting as you riding my dick, sexy as that was, or bossing me around in bed, which granted, is pretty hot, too. Basically, if I'm here with you, and I'm naked, I'm a happy man."

Ben squinted one eye, giving him a skeptical look. "Are you sure you're a real man?"

"As opposed to what? A sex toy?" Gage grinned. "I do have multiple speeds and functions."

Ben rolled his eyes, a smile tugging at his lips. "Yeah, that's what I meant."

"I'm just a guy who likes you, Ben. That's all. Nothing complicated about it."

Gage leaned in and pressed his lips to Ben's neck.

Ben sighed, eyes closing in pleasure. Gage was right. He needed to relax. They'd agreed to date and see where things went. No grand proclamations of love were happening anytime soon, and he couldn't let himself obsess over the small details. If Gage was unsatisfied, he'd have to speak up and let him know.

Just as he began to relax, Gage blew a raspberry against his skin, making Ben shout in surprise and shove him away.

"Stop thinking so hard," Gage said with a grin.

"Oh, you're so done," Ben said, though his laughter ruined the effect of his threat as he launched himself at Gage and attempted to tickle him in retribution.

10

The next few weeks were a blur of "column dates" and lazy afternoons in front of Ben's television and in his bed. He worked nights, so they could only spend evenings together on his days off, but Gage had a more flexible schedule. He managed to stop by every Tuesday afternoon, in addition to his weekends, and Ben was off work Wednesday and Thursday.

Even if all they did most days was eat take-out and watch bad daytime television, Gage never complained.

And the sex continued to be incredible, to Ben's surprise. He'd kind of expected the intensity to wear off, but if going to bed with Gage was going to become mundane, it was going to take more than a few weeks.

Today, Gage had brought over Thai noodles, and they brainstormed about future column dates while they ate.

"Square dancing?" Ben suggested.

Gage laughed. "Oh God. That's not bad. I'll add it to the list."

He leaned forward to write it down, right under diving lessons, adult dodgeball and open mic night with "sing or play guitar?" noted in parentheses.

The longer they did this, the more challenging it was to

come up with dates for Gage's columns. Since roller skating, they'd gone to a poetry slam where Gage had read some epically bad poetry with a grin of apology — and still managed to get a standing ovation. Then, Ben had persuaded him to actually do a knitting workshop. That had been hilarious; Gage's hands were big, which was nice in some contexts, but he was utterly clumsy with knitting needles.

Ben dared to ask the big question that had been burning on his mind lately. "How long does this column series last?"

He was almost afraid of the answer. They hadn't promised each other anything beyond seeing this column series through. At the end of it, they would decide whether they wanted to be together for real. Until that date, Ben was not counting his chickens before they hatched. He was doing his best to withhold his heart.

"Well, it coincides with my class lesson plan, so about two more weeks. Then I'll be more focused on the students' final projects for the semester."

Two weeks.

Ben busied himself clearing away their dishes, so Gage wouldn't see his expression. He knew he was over-reacting. Gage might want to stick around after he was done with the columns. But what if he didn't?

The column series had offered something concrete to hold onto. Ben knew Gage wouldn't break things off until the column series came to an end. That fact had allowed Ben to let his guard down, but he was suddenly afraid that had been a mistake. It was going to hurt *so bad* when it all came crashing to an end.

"I sure will miss our ridiculous dates," Gage said, as if reading his mind.

Ben returned, climbing into Gage's lap and hiding his face in his neck. "And here I thought you liked our afternoons in ..."

"Oh, I do," he said emphatically, grabbing hold of Ben's ass and pulling him in tight.

Ben kissed him, burying his worries and letting his other senses take over. He could still taste the spices from lunch on Gage's tongue.

Gage's breathing sped up as Ben kissed him hard enough he'd forget about their conversation. Heck, if they kept this up, Ben might forget about it himself.

He loved how Gage was so easily affected by his touches. He'd experienced his share of hook-ups, but he'd never had a man turn to putty for him before. It was an intoxicating feeling. This must explain why Gage enjoyed it when Ben melted for him.

They were such a good match in bed. Gage would take charge when Ben needed it, but even though Gage was bigger than him, strong enough to manhandle him, he was equally content to let Ben take the lead.

"Bed?" Gage asked.

"In a minute, professor," Ben said with a wink.

He slid to the floor between Gage's legs, and reached for the button on his jeans. "I've got to earn my A first."

Gage turned red, chuckling a little uncomfortably. "Uh, you know I wouldn't do that with a student."

Ben smiled slyly. "Not even if I were your student?"

He leaned forward, mouthing the bulge in Gage's jeans, which was still hard despite the man's embarrassment. Looking up through his eyelashes, he watched Gage's eyes slip shut.

"Well ..." he trailed off, seemingly unable to find words to answer. "God, Ben, stop teasing me."

"You didn't answer my question."

Gage's eyes opened, foggy with lust. "What was the question?"

"You wouldn't ever do this with a student, even if I were your student?"

"No," Gage answered, making Ben pout that he wouldn't play along. Then he added in a growl, "So don't ever enroll in one of my classes. You're fucking irresistible."

Ben smiled. "That's more like it. I think you earned yourself a blow job, Mr. Evans."

Unzipping Gage's jeans, he grinned as the denim spread to reveal lime green underwear. You wouldn't know it by looking at him, but Gage had a flamboyant side and it resided firmly in his underwear.

Very firmly.

Ben tugged the man's cock out of his underwear and pressed kisses up his shaft. It was his first time doing this for Gage, even though they'd slept together more than a few times by now. Thankfully, he hadn't turned into a pile of goo every time they had sex. He tried to give as good as he got, and most of the time he succeeded, but Gage had a way of overwhelming his senses. Sometimes it was just too intense for Ben to do anything but take whatever Gage gave him.

After getting Gage's cock good and wet with his tongue, he opened his mouth and took it deep on his first try.

"Fuck!"

"Mmm," Ben agreed, humming around Gage's cock and laughing inside when he jerked in pleasure.

Gage's hands found their way into Ben's hair, but he didn't get too pushy. Gage wasn't the only one with great cock-sucking skill. Ben pressed a hand on top of Gage's fingers, pushing down to tell him he could get more assertive.

Gage responded immediately, thrusting up with his hips and pulling Ben's head down at the same time. His cock slid into Ben's throat, blocking his airway for a moment before withdrawing. He tried to time his breaths with Gage's thrusts, letting the man use his mouth at his own tempo.

It didn't take long before Gage's thighs began to tremble under his hands.

Gage abruptly pulled free of his mouth. "I'm going to come if we keep going. Do you want that or ..."

Ben climbed to his feet with a smile and held out a hand. "Let's go to bed."

Gage looked up when his office door opened, fully expecting Chloe to come breezing in. She and her cast had been rehearsing hard as their play date approached, so he hadn't seen a lot of her lately. Ben had helpfully filled the void that her absence usually left in his life.

He still got shivers thinking about the last time he'd been in Ben's bed. The man might be guarded about his feelings and stingy with his trust, but that was one area he let all the walls down.

Gage smiled, but his teasing greeting died on his lips when Zane stepped in looking far too pale and more than a little skittish.

"Hey, Mr. Evans," Zane said, stuffing his hands in his pockets. "Is this an okay time?"

Gage's eyes flicked to the wall clock. Office hours were nearly up, but Ben was having dinner with his mother tonight anyway. Those two were super close, talking on the phone every day and getting together at least two or three times a week. Gage had been secretly hoping Ben might invite him along to one of their get-togethers, but no dice yet.

"It's fine, Zane. Have a seat."

Zane glanced toward the doorway, looking nervous. "Okay if I close the door?"

"Go ahead," Gage said, watching a jittery Zane close the door before slumping into the chair in front of his desk.

"Thanks for seeing me."

"That's what I'm here for," Gage said lightly. "What's going on? You okay?"

Zane rolled his shoulders and took a deep breath. "I'm not sure. Been fighting with my dad."

"About?"

"I'm gay," he said bluntly, "and he doesn't like it. Pretty fucking trite, right? Poor queer kid not being accepted by his parents when he comes out. I'm such a joke."

Gage was a little taken aback by Zane's apparent anger, which seemed to be directed at himself in large part. But he wouldn't be the first person who chose to hate themselves instead of their parents.

"Been out long?" he asked.

Zane seemed surprised by the question. "Just a few weeks."

Gage nodded. "You've always seemed so secure with yourself. I would have guessed you'd been out for years."

Zane sighed and sank back in the chair. "With my friends, sure. But my dad is another story."

"I can understand that. What did he say?"

Zane dropped his head back. Looking at the ceiling, he answered in a hollow voice. "The usual. His son can't be gay, and he won't have a gay son under his roof. He won't pay for a gay son's college tuition. Yadda yadda."

"He threatened to pull your financing?"

"Pretty much a done deal. I told him to fuck himself," Zane said, lifting his head. A small smile curled his lips, despite the sadness coming off him in waves. "Pretty sure this is my last semester, so you can see why I'm not applying myself in class."

"Damn," Gage said, while his brain whirred through options. There was no way he was going to watch a bright kid like Zane drop out of school over something like this.

"We can figure something out," Gage said. "I'll talk to the department head. See if we can get you on a scholarship."

A spark of hope lit in Zane's eyes. "You'd do that?"

"Zane, you're a talented student. You've worked hard. I'm not just going to sit by while you lose your education. We can figure something out to keep you in school."

Zane blew out a relieved breath. "Thanks, man."

"If you want me to talk to your father, I'll do that, too."

Zane's wide eyes jerked up to meet his. "What? No!"

Gage held up his hands as Zane sprang up and started to pace. "It's just an offer. I won't do anything you don't want."

Zane nodded. "Thanks, but ... it's just my dad is an asshole. I'm worried he'll blame you."

"Blame me?"

Zane turned, his cheeks going pink. "Yeah, like say you turned me gay or some bullshit. He's so old-fashioned. Jesus."

"I see. I could maybe see if there's someone else who could talk to him?"

Zane collapsed back into the chair. "Nah, man. Don't. Please."

"Okay, then. Do you have a place to stay?"

Zane nodded, not making eye contact. "I'm crashing with a friend, but I already called my mom. I haven't lived with her since she remarried, but she says it's okay to spend the summer there."

"Have you come out to your mother?"

"Not yet," he said. He nervously drummed his fingers on the arms of his chair. "Not sure if I should now. I mean, I think she'll handle it okay, but what if she rejects me too? I'll have no family."

The pain in his voice resonated with Gage. He didn't know what it was like to grow up with the security of family and have that ripped away. He did know, though, what it was like to feel untethered, watching everyone else go home to a family at night. Celebrate holidays together. Birthdays.

Gage's fingers tightened on the pen he clasped in one hand. He couldn't make this about him.

"You'll always have the family you make. Your friends, your colleagues."

Zane nodded, breathing out a relieved breath, though Gage didn't feel like his words were all that comforting.

"Thanks for listening, and for going to bat for me. You'll let me know what you find out about getting me a scholarship or something?"

"Sure, Zane."

He came around the desk as Zane grabbed his backpack and slung it over one shoulder.

"Just be careful whatever you do, okay?" he said. "Call me if you need anything."

Zane nodded, keeping his eyes on the floor, and Gage couldn't stand to watch it. He tugged Zane in for a hug, and the kid clung to him, breathing hard like he was trying not to cry.

"You're gonna be okay," Gage said quietly, as he rubbed a soothing hand on his back. "You're not some LGBT cliché, okay? Everything's going to work out."

Zane cleared his throat and drew back, swiping at his face. "Thanks, man. I should go."

Gage nodded, understanding Zane's reluctance to meet his eye as he left the office. It was hard to make yourself vulnerable.

Zane had swallowed his pride to come here and talk about his problems. Gage respected him for that.

11

"**K**araoke? Tell me you're kidding."

"Nope." Gage's grin was wide, the kind of joyful expression that was utterly contagious. "You didn't want dangerous, so ..."

"You're so funny," Ben deadpanned.

Gage chuckled. "It's about living in the moment, this series of columns. Besides, I'm dying to hear your singing voice and you vetoed the open mic night."

"You might die when you hear it," Ben muttered.

Ben gave Gage a hard time, but truthfully doing this series of "dates" for Gage's columns had been the most fun Ben had experienced in months, if not years. He loved his work as a nurse, but at some point, he'd let it become his whole life. All other interests had fallen to the wayside, and one by one, his friends had dropped away.

Some of them moved for jobs; some of them got married and started raising kids. He couldn't even say exactly how or when it happened, just that one day he woke up, and the only people in his social circle were other nurses and his mother.

Thank God for his mom.

They'd done a movie and dinner the night before, watching one of the sappy rom-coms his mom loved so much. Ben didn't *hate* them, but he was more of a comedy kind of guy. In the short time he'd been seeing Gage, he'd already figured out he was an action/adventure kind of movie fan. It was so predictable it was almost funny, but somehow Gage's predictability was a comfort rather than an irritation.

Karaoke. Maybe he *should* have predicted that. Gage had been ridiculously in favor of the open mic night, but only if Ben participated (unlike the poetry slam, where Ben had flat-out refused). He'd vetoed it, but told Gage he could pick anything else on the list. He'd forgotten about the damned karaoke.

He followed Gage into the lounge of a bar that had clearly made karaoke night its big claim to fame. A stage was positioned at one end, and Ben hoped they at least got some real bands in once in a while to use it. On the wall beside it was a large screen where he expected they projected the words to the songs.

Karaoke hadn't started yet, so the bar piped pop songs through the speaker system. Most people were sitting at tables in little groups, munching on appetizers and drinking beer. It had the casual vibe of a sports bar without all the televisions and sports paraphernalia on the walls. Ben supposed it could be worse; at least it wasn't some pretentious dance club with colored strobes. He hated that crap.

"So, what made you decide to do this?" he asked after they were both settled with their drinks. Beers for them both; wheat beer made by a local brewer for Gage, who was a bit of a connoisseur, and plain old Budweiser for Ben. He wasn't a big beer drinker, but he didn't want to cope with the aftermath of hard liquor.

"What, karaoke? I already said—"

"No, the whole series. The experience life series or whatever you call it."

Gage smirked. "Guess that tells me how often you read my columns, huh? I named the series The Bucket List, actually."

"I read them," Ben protested. "You send them all to me before they print, though." He ducked his head, feeling a little ashamed. "I don't buy the paper."

Gage laughed. "You and about 75 percent of this town. That's just the fate of local newspapers. But to answer your question, the reason I'm doing the column series is in the name. It's kind of a bucket list for me."

"Skateboarding was on your bucket list?"

Ben's eyebrow ticked up. He knew he sounded incredulous, but he couldn't help it. His own bucket list would have items like "travel to Greece."

Gage pointed his bottle at Ben. "I know what you're thinking." He laughed. "I guess I didn't get a lot of teen adventure, and it's not like I can go climb Mount Everest for a local column."

"Is that something you'd want to do?"

"Nah, not really. I'm not outdoorsy enough."

"So, why didn't you get more adventure as a teen?"

Ben knew he was asking twenty questions, but he couldn't help his curiosity about Gage. There was still so much he didn't know about him, and he felt like he was running out of time. Tonight was the next to last column "date," and Ben was queasy with the uncertainty that waited ahead.

Would Gage want to continue dating? Or would he tell Ben what so many others had before? *"Hey, it's been fun, but I just can't see a future with you."*

It had been easier to push away his doubts and fears when they had the rest of the column series stretching ahead of them. Ben could just tell himself to think about it *later*. To talk to Gage *later*. To ask Gage to share something of his feelings, *much later*.

Well, *later* was *now*. The clock was ticking down and Ben was no closer to knowing what was in Gage's mind. And even if Gage suddenly turned to him right now and said every-thing Ben longed to hear — *"Let's keep dating"* or *"Let's try to make a life together"* — Ben didn't know if he could trust the words.

He'd been burned so many times.

Gage was so extroverted and adventurous, though, that Ben couldn't imagine why he wouldn't have done any of the things on this "Bucket List" of his before. He watched Gage, waiting for the answer to his question. *Why didn't he experience more of these things when he was younger?*

Gage shrugged a shoulder. "I don't know. Moved around a lot. Never had the opportunity, I guess."

He raised his bottle, taking a long drink. There was some-thing about the dismissal that didn't ring true, or if true, then incomplete.

Ben leaned forward in his seat. "So, why—"

"They're getting ready to start," Gage said, and seconds later there was a good deal of hooting and hollering to confirm he was right and not trying to divert Ben. Or not only trying to divert him anyway.

"I better go grab the book or we'll never get up there."

Ben nodded, watching Gage join the cluster of people seeking out the book of songs. He was joking with the guy next to him, looking incredibly confident and sexy, and Ben resolved to let go of his questions for a night. He could draw Gage out another time.

Tonight, he'd let him have his life experience, as godawful as it might be, and revel in the pleasure of being with him.

However short-lived it might be.

After 45 minutes of chatting and laughing at the atrocious acts hitting the stage, their turn arrived, and Gage dragged Ben onto the stage.

Ben played up his reluctance: dragging his feet, looking around anxiously and mumbling, "What the hell have I gotten myself into?"

Gage saw past all that. Underneath his protests, Ben secretly wanted to get out there and enjoy life.

They stumbled onto the stage. They'd both had several more beers, freely acknowledging they needed liquid courage to sing publicly. They'd haggled long and hard over the songs, but had finally decided on "I Will Survive" by Gloria Gaynor. After all, who didn't know that song? And it wasn't the kind of thing that required a strong singing voice.

There were at least a couple of people in the crowd who took their karaoke seriously. They looked like college students, so they were probably music majors who enjoyed singing publicly. They chose ballads that showcased their voices, and yeah, they could sing, but they weren't taking home a record deal anytime soon.

A crowd-pleaser like "I Will Survive" would be way more fun.

They jostled for space in front of the screen where they could follow the lyrics as the music started. Ben was grinning, brown eyes warm and melty. Gage was grinning too, but it was his insides turning melty.

What was it about this guy?

The first line came up, and they launched into the song.

Gage was pretty drunk, so it actually took him a while to realize that while he was bellowing the lyrics, Ben was singing with perfect pitch. Halfway through the song, Gage trailed off and just watched Ben work the stage.

Gone was the nurse. Ben opened his mouth wide, projecting his notes across the room like a pro. He approached the front of the stage, leaning forward to blow kisses at his adoring fans, mostly a whole lot of drunk college kids and twenty-somethings.

Remembering that Chloe was in the crowd, Gage scanned for her. He spotted her close to the front of the crowd with Adam and Bella from the cast, cheering for Ben and giving Gage a not-so-subtle two thumbs up. He assumed that was her way of telling him he'd picked a winner.

As the song wound down, Gage's eyes were drawn to a guy right up front by the stage. Zane was there, with a couple of other people Gage had never met. A girl and a guy who appeared to be dating, judging by how they hung on each other.

He was surprised to see Zane, especially because the student wasn't old enough to drink. Yet in his hand was a half-empty beer bottle.

As Gage watched, Zane licked his lips and blew a kiss directly at Ben.

And Ben reciprocated.

What the fuck?

Ben was high on adrenaline as the song wrapped up. He turned to share his enthusiasm with Gage, but he was already on the stairs. He realized, belatedly, that Gage hadn't been singing for the last part of the song.

He followed him down, wondering if he'd done something to piss him off, but when Gage glanced back over his shoulder he was smiling. *Must be my imagination.*

When he reached the floor, Gage leaned in to be heard over the noise of the bar.

"Want another drink? I thought we could join Chloe's crowd. I think she wants to cast you in her next musical."

Ben laughed. "Sure, get me a beer. I'll pay you back later."

"No worries."

Gage made his way through the crowd toward the bar, and Ben turned to scan the room for Chloe and company. Before he spotted them, the fun guy from the crowd who'd been helping Ben work the stage popped up in front of him.

He leaned in close to Ben's ear to speak, but pretty much everyone did that because it was so noisy.

"You were great, Ben!"

Ben took a second look at the cute, dark-haired guy and a memory clicked. "You're the student, right? From the ER with Gage?"

"Zane," he said, flashing a big smile. "Your voice is really incredible."

Ben laughed. "It's less incredible when you're not drunk."

Zane snorted. "No, really. I don't think it's the beer making you sound so sexy." His eyes made a slow slide over Ben from head to toe. "You look pretty good, too."

Ben couldn't help the surprised flush of pleasure that went through him. Zane was cute, with the kind of charisma that reached out and grabbed you.

The thought flitted through his mind that he didn't know where things with Gage were going. If he was going to keep himself from getting in any deeper, he shouldn't shy away from some harmless flirting. Hell, he should probably hook up with at least one other guy so he didn't shatter when things came to an end. Better to draw away now, painful as it was, than have everything ripped from him at once.

"You're too sweet, Zane," he said, performing his own sweep of Zane's body. He had a runner's build, more slender than Gage or Ben, but he had nice muscle definition in his arms.

Zane grinned, and his dark eyes sparked with mischief. "You're pretty sweet yourself, Nurse Ben."

Ben glanced over his shoulder, spotting Chloe and her group

at a table in the corner. "I was about to go meet some friends. You can join us, if you want."

Zane placed a hand on Ben's waist, while leaning in close to speak in his ear. "You sure you don't want to find a quieter spot?"

Ben became aware of how close they were, their chests brushing as Zane's breath whispered across his neck. The hand on his waist tightened, burning like a brand through his shirt.

"Oh. Um."

Ben's brain reached for an answer, while guilt unfurled in his chest. *This is why you don't flirt!*

It was all harmless fun until you were sucking some guy off in the parking lot. And this wasn't just some guy. It was Zane, Gage's student. That would be double the betrayal.

Which was when it hit him. He could never sleep with another guy while seeing Gage, even casually. It would hurt Gage, and Ben couldn't bring himself to do that.

He'd have to find a way to protect his heart, but this wasn't it.

He shook his head. "Zane, you're cute, but—"

A beer bottled was thrust between them, forcing Zane back a step.

Ben looked up to see Gage's furious eyes fixed on them.

"Here," Gage said abruptly, pushing the bottle into his chest and letting go so Ben had no choice but to grab the beer before it landed on the floor.

"I didn't mean to interrupt. I'll let you two finish your chat."

Sarcasm dripped from his words, and Ben couldn't miss the flare of hurt in his eyes before he turned on his heel and pushed his way across the room.

Zane gave Ben an apologetic smile. "Sorry, I didn't know it was serious between you guys."

Ben thought about objecting. They hadn't made any promises, not even exclusivity. But it seemed like too much trouble to explain it. Not to mention it *felt* like a lie. He didn't know what they were doing, or how long they would last, but he knew Gage wouldn't choose to be with another guy while they were together.

"I better go," he said, turning to follow Gage.

Watching the rigid line of Gage's shoulders move through the crowd, Ben wasn't sure whether to feel guilty or angry at the man's display of jealousy.

Ben hadn't actually done anything wrong, *wouldn't* have taken Zane up on his offer. But he *had* considered briefly the idea he should mess around with another guy, and just the memory of that left a bad taste in his mouth.

Gage's fuming jealousy helped him push away the feeling of guilt. It seemed Ben wasn't the only one with trust issues – the only difference being, he'd been honest about his hang-ups and Gage hadn't.

───

Ben joined him at Chloe's table, and Gage did his best to pretend his ego wasn't smarting. He knew Ben wasn't ready to be in a serious relationship, but he didn't think Ben would flirt with another guy right under his nose, either. *Why had it been so hard to get Ben's interest when it was obviously pretty easy for Zane?*

"Ben, you've been holding out on us!" Chloe exclaimed as soon as he sat down. "That was in key and everything."

Ben blushed, looking bashful at the praise. He was fucking adorable, so Gage looked away. He wasn't ready to let go of his anger, and if he looked at Ben too long, he wouldn't be able to help himself.

"It wasn't a difficult song."

Ben deflected the compliments, as he so often did. Usually, Gage found that endearing. Tonight, it just grated on his nerves.

If Ben couldn't accept a compliment, how would he ever

accept Gage's love? Not that he'd used the L word with Ben. He didn't want to send the man jack-rabbiting again.

"That didn't stop Gage from belting out the lyrics in three different keys, none of which were the right one."

Chloe nudged him in the ribs, and Gage forced a weak smile. "I try."

Adam leaned in close to Chloe, whispering in her ear. A smile spread across her face and she nodded.

"Yeah, sign me up."

Gage watched the exchange and for the briefest moment, his irritation with Ben was forgotten. *The spark in her eye, and that smile ...*

Adam stood up and headed for the stage, and Gage turned a pointed gaze on her. She caught his eye and flushed with guilt.

He wanted to drag her from the table and get the full story from her, but he didn't want to leave Ben there. He didn't want Zane to have any opportunities to take another shot at his guy. Also, he wasn't entirely sure Ben wouldn't just up and leave.

Even though Gage was the one who should be upset, every time he caught a glimpse of Ben, he looked pissed as hell.

Gage switched to water, sensing they might need to leave sooner rather than later. Lost in his own chaotic thoughts, he let the conversation flow around him, but when an opportunity presented itself, he leaned over to hiss in Chloe's ear.

"Adam? Really?"

"Shut up, Gage," she snapped, confirming his suspicions.

She glanced around the table, where most everyone else was caught up in the their own conversations.

She spoke low into his ear. "Adam's not some kid. He's 25. And we're being discreet."

"That is such a bad idea."

"Yeah, well, you have your own problems to deal with, don't you?"

She nodded her head toward Ben, who was sitting with his arms crossed over his chest, staring out toward the karaoke stage – though no one was performing right now. His jaw was clenched so tightly no one would miss the anger coursing through him.

She was right. He didn't want to be here, with all this tension between them.

He kissed Chloe's cheek. "Just be careful."

"I will."

Turning, he nudged Ben. "Want to get out of here?"

Ben nodded without a word.

After saying their goodbyes, they found their way to the door and outside into the fresh air. They didn't linger but made for Gage's silver Infiniti, parked toward the back of the lot.

Once inside, Gage leaned over the center console and kissed Ben long and hard.

He was still angry, but he also felt the need to assert his place in Ben's world. He kissed Ben. No one else.

Ben was resistant at first, but he softened before long, one hand snaking up into Gage's hair and curling there. Gage loved the feel of Ben's hands in his hair, pulling him closer, and the small sound of pleasure he made in the back of his throat when their tongues touched.

When they were intimate like this, he had no doubts about Ben's feelings for him. The rest of the time, though, Ben was tough to read. His walls were tall and thick and so far, Gage was still on the outside.

He pulled away and started the car, heading in the direction of Ben's house. They'd mostly spent their nights together there because Ben liked to keep an eye on Bruiser. The cat was still stand-offish, but he was far less feral and very slowly warming up to Ben.

Gage had planned to take Ben to bed and try to forget the

situation in the bar. But he couldn't get that image out of his head: Zane and Ben pressed together, Zane's hands where Gage's belonged, his lips too close to the sensitive spot under Ben's ear.

The words that had been eating at him ever since he saw them together flew out of his mouth uncensored.

"So, what the fuck was that with the flirting in front of my face?" he asked.

Ben huffed, sounding annoyed. "It was hardly in front of your face," he said sarcastically. "More like behind your back."

"Are you trying to be funny right now?"

"Yeah, Gage," Ben deadpanned. "This whole thing is hilarious."

Gage hated it when Ben went all smart-ass. That was usually a tell-tale sign the wall was going up in a hurry.

"You know, Ben, I knew you weren't ready for something serious. You're still messed up over the biker. I get that, and I was willing to be patient. But waiting for you, and watching you fuck around with other guys are two different things."

They rolled to a stop at a traffic light, and Gage looked over to see Ben's eyes snapping with fury.

"You call this patient? We're sleeping together. We're dating. You wanted me, and you got me, even after I warned you I wasn't ready for it."

A small niggle of guilt squirmed in Gage's chest. Had he pushed Ben too far too fast? He thought he'd been taking this at Ben's pace, but maybe not.

"You did warn me," Gage said. "I thought we were finally on the same page, but maybe I was wrong. Maybe I should just give up."

"You want to give up?"

Ben's voice was suddenly vulnerable, the anger of a moment ago gone.

Gage saw pain twist his features before he turned his face to the window. The light turned green, and Gage made the turn down Ben's quiet street. At this hour, the road was empty and that somehow magnified the chasm rising up between them.

A lump rose in Gage's throat, and he had to fight past it to get his words out.

"No, I don't want to give up, but ..."

"I'm not giving you what you want, right? You want my heart on a platter, so you can tear into it. But I'm not that guy anymore. I'm not just handing my heart over—"

"Jesus Christ, do you hear yourself, Ben? I'm not going to carve up your heart and eat it. Can't I get just the smallest amount of trust?"

He pulled the car into Ben's drive and turned off the engine. They sat in tense silence for a long minute. A million different phrases swam through Gage's mind, and he discarded them one by one without speaking.

I'm sorry.

I love you.

You're carving up my heart, Ben. I have a heart, too!

"I want to trust you," Ben whispered finally. "I just don't know if I can."

Gage nodded. He stared out the windshield, into the dark landscape, unable to look at Ben. He knew what he had to do, but it hurt like hell.

"Well, until you do, I think maybe ... we should stop seeing each other."

Ben sucked in a shaky breath. His voice, when it came, trembled between them.

"I guess I always knew this day would come."

Gage turned, anger burning through his disappointment. "No, you thought I'd break your heart. This is you breaking mine."

Ben's eyes widened. "What?"

Gage's voice rasped painfully as he held back his emotion through strength of will.

"All I wanted was you. Don't you get that? I can't watch you toy with me, push me away, hook up with random guys—"

"I wasn't going to hook up!"

"Even so. You thought about it. I watched you think about it, so don't lie to me."

"I was flattered! That doesn't mean I was going to do anything. I can't believe you're this pissed over some harmless flirting! You obviously don't trust me, either."

"Maybe I don't," Gage acknowledged. "I have my own issues, Ben. You're not the only one with a past. But I try not to let it define me." He stopped short of adding *unlike you.* No doubt Ben could sense the unspoken words.

"What issues?"

"I was a foster kid. I had a screwed up childhood, and I've got no family besides Chloe. That's why I'm doing this column, why I never got to go skateboarding or roller skating when I was a kid. I moved around too much, and usually the foster families didn't want to spend their money on a kid who might be gone in a matter of weeks or months."

"I didn't know that."

Gage's hands tightened on the steering wheel. "I don't like to think about it," he admitted. "I try not to let it get in the way of my life, but how can I give you *my* trust when you're always pulling away from me?"

"I don't know."

"I'm serious about you, Ben. I don't want casual. I want you and me together, planning a future. I want you to trust me with your heart, not worry I'm going to tear it to pieces. Until you can do that, we're only going to hurt each other. So ... I think it's best we take a break."

Ben bit down on his lip, looking torn. "Gage ... "

Gage shook his head and leaned over to kiss him softly.

"Decide what you really want and what you can handle, and then let me know. I'm sorry, but I have a heart to protect, too."

Ben nodded, blinking fast. "I'm sorry."

Gage squeezed his hand. "I know."

Ben opened the door and stepped out, and Gage forced himself to turn the ignition instead of jumping out to follow Ben and beg for his love. His chest was tight, crammed too full of emotion and yet strangely empty at the same time.

The car door closed, and he watched Ben walked up his sidewalk, unlock his door, and go inside.

Ben hesitated in the entrance, staring in Gage's direction. Then he shook his head and closed the door.

It was over, for now. Only time would tell if it was over for good.

Ben was shaking when he stepped through the front door. His eyes burned and his throat ached. It was only through sheer will he'd kept his emotions in check with Gage.

Now, he was alone. His house echoed its absence of another person in the easily heard hum of a refrigerator.

The creak of a settling foundation.

The sound of his breath hitching as the first sob broke free.

"Oh God," he gasped.

Gage was gone.

Ben stumbled to the couch and dropped onto a cushion. His eyes blurred with tears, and his chest ached.

"Your fault. It's your fault. Why, why, why! Why did you do that?"

All his regrets, all the words he couldn't get out when Gage was still within his grasp, tumbled out in a series of sobs and incoherent moans.

Meow.

Bruiser slunk in from the dining room and paused to stretch. *Meow?*

The cat sounded more plaintive than angry for once.

Ben became aware he was clutching his chest. He moved his hand to mop at a face wet with tears and snot.

Bruiser jumped onto the couch next to him, shocking the hell out of him. He must look a mess if the most distant pet ever took an interest.

"What are we going to do?" Ben asked Bruiser.

The cat stepped onto his lap, and he obediently stroked Bruiser's head when nudged.

"Gage was practically perfect. I mean, he couldn't sing to save his life and he's clumsy and gets injured way too often, but I—"

He stopped, heart thundering.

"Oh shit," he whispered. "I love him."

All that effort to keep Gage at arm's length. All that work to hold back pieces of himself. *Pointless.*

His heart clenched in his chest, as if to remind him of the heartbreak he'd failed to avoid.

Bruiser's purr startled him. He looked down at the once feral cat, now kneading his thigh —painfully, he noticed, as he became aware of the world around him once more.

He pried a paw loose.

Bruiser's purr rumbled like an engine in need of a tune-up.

"I'm glad one of us is happy."

Bruiser gazed up at him intently. His purr faded behind a meow that seemed to ask, "You okay?"

Ben rolled his eyes at himself.

"I bet you want your dinner," he said, shifting in his seat.

Bruiser jumped to the floor and ran toward the kitchen, proving he was the same self-centered feline, not the adoring kitty Ben had imagined for a brief moment.

But when Ben went to bed, quieter tears soaking into his pillow, Bruiser slept on the pillow beside him for the first time.

12

Gage woke to a pounding on his front door. The bedroom was still dark, and his internal clock was telling him it was too early for visitors.

He checked the time on his phone. 6 a.m. *What the fuck?*

Stretching, he felt the cold sheets beside him, and it all came rushing back. He was in his bed alone, instead of with Ben, because ... *fuck.* He'd told Ben they should call it quits until he was ready to commit and trust.

The knocking resumed on the front door, and his heart leapt in his chest. Maybe that was Ben. Maybe he'd come over to tell Gage that he didn't want to lose him. That he was ready for a serious relationship.

He jumped out of bed, tripping over his tangled sheets, and then ran for the front door. Without pausing to look through the small window, he yanked the door open.

"Hey ..."

The hope died in his chest.

Standing on his porch was a wide-eyed Chloe holding two coffees and reeking of beer and other scents he didn't want to identify.

"Don't look so happy to see me," she said, brushing past him without waiting for an invitation.

Gage closed the door, and she held out a coffee.

"Brought you a spicy mocha," she said in that trilling voice that told him he was being buttered up for something. His eyes narrowed.

"Why?"

"Because you like them?"

"No." He crossed his arms over his chest, just now becoming aware he was standing there in nothing more than banana yellow briefs.

Chloe's smirk indicated she'd noticed his barely dressed state and was waiting for him to realize himself and get embarrassed. Annoyed, he pretended he didn't care that he was more than half-naked.

"Why are you here at 6 a.m., crazy woman? And why are you buttering me up with my favorite coffee?"

Her lips pouted. "I thought we should talk."

His eyebrow arched. He smelled bullshit. "Try again."

"Okay," she said with a groan and flopped down on his couch. "I'm doing the walk of shame. Adam lives down the block, and I need a ride to my car. Please?"

Gage stared at her, taking in that she was wearing the same clothes as the night before.

"Did he kick you out before you'd even showered?" He sat his coffee cup on the end table, and turned for his room. "Let me get dressed, and I'll go kick his ass."

Chloe jumped up and grabbed his arm. "No! No, it's not him. I crept out while he was sleeping."

He turned to eye her. "Why would you do that?"

She cringed. "I looked over, and I didn't see the sexy man I went to bed with. You know what I saw?"

He shook his head.

"A *student*. I slept with a student, Gage. I'm a freaking cliché!"

"But you knew that last night."

"Yeah, well, alcohol." She shrugged. "Bad judgment and hormones. You know how it goes. So what do you say? Can you take me to my car?"

He sighed. "Let me get dressed."

A few minutes later, in significantly more clothing, Gage climbed into his car with Chloe and headed back toward the bar where he'd spent his last date with Ben.

Chloe chattered about anything and everything except her impulsive jump into bed with Adam, and Gage didn't push her.

"Gage? Are you listening?"

"Hmm?"

He jerked his attention back to the woman in the car. She was staring at him speculatively. He didn't like that look. Nothing good ever came of it.

"So, Ben wasn't at your place."

"Nope."

"You guys have a love spat?"

Gage laughed, unable to contain the bitter sound that erupted. "That's an understatement."

He'd spent a long, restless night after dropping off Ben after karaoke. God, that tense car ride might be the last time he ever saw the man he loved. What the hell had he been thinking?

"So, you'll make up," Chloe said. "Everyone fights."

Gage snorted. "I wish it were so simple. We broke up."

"What did you do?" Chloe asked immediately, sounding accusing.

"Why does it have to be my fault?"

"This is Ben we're talking about. He's a sweetheart."

"Maybe to you," Gage mumbled.

"Okay, out with it. The whole story. Now."

When Chloe used that commanding tone, there was no

arguing. Gage reluctantly filled her in on Ben's wariness about dating and his low self-esteem issues that kept him from trusting Gage.

"So, you gave him an ultimatum," she said, after he'd finished summarizing the argument from the night before.

Gage groaned. "Stupid, right? I should have been patient, but he was flirting with one of my students and I lost it."

Chloe scoffed. "Ben is gorgeous. Men and women will try to flirt with him. It doesn't mean he's going to do anything. If you want to be with him, you're going to have to trust him too."

"But we're not exclusive. He wanted to keep it casual."

Gage pulled into the bar parking lot and stopped next to Chloe's car. Cutting the engine, he turned to see a skeptical expression on her face.

"What?" he asked.

She shrugged. "He may say that, but Ben doesn't feel casual about you."

That gave Gage pause. Could it be that if he'd ignored Ben's words and trusted him to follow his heart, they could have gotten through this? It hardly mattered now. Maybe if he hadn't walked away, but Ben would only come back now if his mind and his heart were in sync.

"Fuck. How do you know that?"

She hummed as she thought. "He watches you all the time. And with so much affection. This is Ben we're talking about. The guy's brown eyes are so warm he makes me crave chocolate."

"You always crave chocolate."

She laughed. "Lies."

Gage sighed. "What can I do? I don't want to lose him."

"You should have though of that before cutting him loose."

He bristled. "Aren't you supposed to be my friend? Seems like you should say 'good job for not staying with a guy who doesn't trust you' or 'it's good you're not sacrificing what you want for a relationship that might fail.' "

"I *am* your friend, which is why I'm not wasting time telling you what you want to hear. From your accounts, Ben was skittish from the beginning. He warned you off again and again and you wanted to take the gamble. Now, you've folded when the game is just getting started. You know why you did that?"

"I'm sure you'll tell me."

"Because you were okay risking Ben's trust, but now that your heart is in the game, you don't want to play so loose and fast anymore. And now you know how he's felt the whole time."

"Scared as fuck?"

"Yep."

"Damn." He sighed and ran a hand through his hair. "What if I can't fix it?"

She reached for the door handle, but paused before getting it out. "You *will* fix it, or I'll kick your ass."

He laughed. "Stellar advice."

She winked. "I'm full of it."

"You're full of something," he said.

She scowled and slid out of the seat. As she circled his car to head to her own, he rolled down the window and called her over.

"Hey, Chloe!"

She bent down to look through the window. "What now?"

"You were right last night. Adam is not a kid. He might be a student, but he's also a grown man. Call him, and tell him you're sorry for sneaking out like a skank."

Her mouth dropped open, and she slapped his arm. "I'm not a skank!"

Gage grinned. "Just call him. If the student thing bothers you, tell him to give you a call after graduation. Just ... don't blow it if you think this could be the real thing."

She nodded and reached in to tousle his hair. "Okay, as long as you follow your own advice."

He waited while she got in her car and pulled out of the lot, then headed home to get ready for work. As much as he didn't want to deal with life right now, his class would be there at 9 a.m., ready to talk about their final project of the semester.

Zane would be there, too.

Shit.

Gage saw Zane approaching after class and hurried to scoop his papers into his satchel so he could escape.

He had hoped Zane might skip his class, as fucked up as that was, but for once, the student had been on time and attentive throughout the discussion of their final alternative journalism projects, which would involve them writing a final – and much longer – article about the past several weeks experiencing an activity out of their comfort zone.

Gage had approved the topics himself, pushing the students to truly choose activities they had no prior experience with. The one sorority girl in the class was participating in a robotics club that built competition bots and mostly included a lot of engineering students, and Trent, one of the guys that came to class half-baked and wearing grungy clothes, was hanging out with one of the preppy political groups on campus.

Zane had difficulty choosing an assignment, but they'd finally agreed that he could spend his time with an a Capella group, even rehearsing and performing with them. Gage knew this was out of his comfort zone, even though he had a good voice, because Zane liked to be the wise-ass in the back of the room far more than the guy in front of everyone's eyes.

That might explain why he'd been at karaoke, come to think

of it. There'd been a couple of college choir singers there who took themselves a bit too seriously.

He was still angry at Zane for hitting on Ben and angry at himself for giving Ben an ultimatum. He wanted to believe Ben would come back to him, but he really didn't know if he would.

"Can I talk to you?" Zane called as Gage turned for the door.

He stopped, unable to bring himself to ignore a student, but he couldn't raise even the semblance of a polite smile.

"Maybe you should make an appointment to visit me during office hours," he said.

"It will only take a second. Please?"

Gage glanced around, noting the room had mostly emptied out. Watching the last lingering students chatter their way out the door, he schooled his face to remain professional before turning to Zane.

"Fine. Let's hear it."

"I'm so, so sorry about what happened at the bar."

Gage bit down on his anger. Ben was the one who was in a relationship with him — or not, as it were — not Zane. He was just an immature kid.

He'd disappointed Gage, though. He'd tried to help Zane through a tough time and he got no respect in return.

"What exactly are you sorry about?"

Zane looked uncomfortable. "Well, the thing with Ben ... and, you know, hitting on him. I didn't know you guys were together for real."

Gage didn't believe that for a second.

"We were there together," he pointed out. "We were on stage together, though by the way you watched him maybe you didn't notice."

"Gage, I didn't mean—"

"Mr. Evans," he corrected.

"Mr. Evans, right, sorry. Look, I messed up. I was drunk and stupid. This thing with my family—"

His voice broke, and Gage was reminded that Zane was in self-destruct mode. He'd been slipping at school – turning in work late or not at all – but Gage thought he'd gotten Zane back on track with his offer to help search for scholarships. He'd already talked to the head of the communications department, and there were several scholarships up for grabs for the next semester. No promises were made, but Zane's talent assured Gage he would easily win one or more of them if he tried.

But maybe there was more to his behavior than a fear he couldn't return to school. Being rejected by someone you loved was a terrible thing. Gage felt ripped to shreds over Ben, and they'd only been together a short time. To have your own parent do that to you ... well, Gage couldn't really relate. He could only imagine. He was young enough when he lost his mom he had only vague memories of the pain he felt that she didn't try to get him back after child services removed him from their home. A part of him had always known the drugs came first.

Gage realized this thing with Ben was just one more way for Zane to torpedo his life.

He sighed, unable to hold on to his anger but also not ready to be the comforting mentor Zane needed.

"You should talk to someone," he said at last. "Find a friend or a teacher you trust, okay? You'll be able to win some scholarships for next semester. I have no doubt you'll be okay there, Zane. But if you continue the way you have been, you're going to destroy what you have going for you."

Zane looked disappointed. "Maybe I could come by during office hours again and we could talk?"

Gage shook his head. "I don't think I'm the right person to help you," he said. "Not right now anyway. I've got my own problems. My head isn't in the right place."

He didn't say his problems revolved around Ben, but Zane was a smart kid. He winced, guilt swamping his features.

"I fucked up. I'm sorry."

Gage managed a nod of acceptance, if not any words.

"I hope I didn't mess up everything with you and Ben."

Gage wasn't able to be the objective mentor Zane needed, but his anger had fizzled out. Zane had enough problems without feeling guilty about Gage's relationship fail.

"We did that all by ourselves," he said. "Don't worry about that."

13

Ben dug through the supplies, grumbling to himself about the chaos on the shelf before him. They organized this every damn night, and every night someone was sloppy and rushed and made their job more difficult.

He'd spent a lot of time in the storage room over the past few days. He was a zombie at work, stumbling through the motions and doing his best to put on a good face for his patients while avoiding his co-workers as much as possible. Alex knew he and Gage were over – he couldn't avoid giving her at least that much information – but he'd been dodging looks of pity and attempts to talk about it ever since.

The storage room was his one respite – no looks, no words, no obligations. He could dart in there for a few quiet minutes, reorganize a few shelves and pull himself back together. But he couldn't stay too long. The job was far too demanding for that.

He moved the box of sterile gloves back to where they belonged, pulling two pairs out – one to wear and one to stuff in his waistband for later – and braced himself to return to his rounds.

Ben became aware of someone behind him a second before warmth pressed against his back.

"Slow night, if you've got time to clean up in here."

Ben recognized Dr. Johnston's voice immediately. He spoke close to Ben's ear, while leaning past him to grab a couple of plastic syringes.

"It's not too crazy," Ben said, stepping to the side so they wouldn't be touching.

He wasn't sure what to make of Dr. Johnston's comment. *Was he implying Ben was wasting his time in here?*

"I heard you broke up with your boyfriend," Dr. Johnston said.

"News travels fast," Ben said quietly, but inside he was fuming. Alex hadn't wasted any time spreading that around the hospital.

"I overheard a couple of nurses talking," Dr. Johnston said. "They were worried about you."

"Well, I'm fine."

Ben looked down at the pair of sterile gloves in his hands while he tried to come up with a polite way to extricate himself from the conversation. He didn't want or need Dr. Johnston's sympathy. He just wanted to focus on his job, and forget about Gage for a few hours.

It would be a lot easier if they were busier, he thought, and immediately felt bad. Busy equaled ill or injured people, and he wouldn't wish that on anyone.

Fingers touched his face, and he startled, looking up at Dr. Johnston. "You know, I've been interested in you for a while. Now that you're single ..."

"No," Ben said sharply, and the doctor took a quick step back.

"Wow, you didn't have to think about that long," he said bitterly.

Ben shook his head, his eyes darting to the ring on Dr. Johnston's ring finger. The man caught his gaze, and rubbed the ring with his thumb.

"I'm getting divorced," he offered. "We're already separated."

Fair enough, but Ben still wasn't interested. *Was there something in the water?* He went weeks before he met Gage without the slightest sign of interest from anyone. Now, both Zane and the doctor had hit on him and he couldn't possibly be less interested.

Dr. Johnston took a step toward him, and Ben held up a hand to stop him. "Whether you're married or not, I love my boyfriend and this is totally inappropriate."

He faltered for a moment at his own words. *Was* Gage his boyfriend? Was there any salvaging their relationship from the mess he'd made of it? He didn't know, and right now he had to deal with a doctor who was looking decidedly put out.

Dr. Johnston started to protest. "But if you broke up—"

"I agree," a voice said from the doorway. "This is not appropriate."

Ben whipped his head around to see Alex standing there, eyes narrowed on Dr. Johnston with immense dislike.

"Dr. Johnston, I think it would be best for you to leave now," she added.

The doctor exchanged a nervous glance between Ben and Alex. He lifted his hands in a placating manner.

"Sorry," he said. "We got our wires crossed, but no harm done. Right?"

He smiled at Ben beseechingly, and Ben didn't have the energy to turn this into some sort of workplace drama. He had enough drama to cope with at the moment.

He nodded. "Right."

Alex waited while Dr. Johnston made his way out of the storage room, then turned on Ben.

"What the hell was that?"

His eyebrows shot up. "That was the result of your big mouth telling everyone I broke up with Gage!"

"I didn't tell anyone," she insisted. "Dawn was worried about you. I said you were having some problems with your boyfriend, but I never gave out any details or said you guys broke up. I swear."

"Well, he heard it somewhere."

"Wishful thinking, more like. You really ought to file a complaint—"

Ben groaned, raising his hands to cover his face. It's not like the doctor had assaulted him. He'd made a play, but he'd respected Ben's refusal, even if he didn't like it.

"I can't deal with this right now."

"Fair enough," Alex said, and he dropped his hands to look at her, surprised she'd let it go so easily. "There's someone here asking for you. He's in Exam 2, and you need to go see him."

Something in her tone made his blood freeze. He snapped his gaze up to her.

"It's not...?"

She shook her head. "It's not Gage. It's the other one, the young guy that was with him once. I think."

Ben felt an irrational surge of anger when he thought of Zane. It wasn't the kid's fault that Ben flirted with him, messing up things with Gage. He should have told Zane he wasn't available. Instead, he'd let his insecurities ruin a good thing.

"Why's he here?"

Alex handed over the chart without a word. Ben flipped it open to scan the details recorded, and then cursed under his breath.

"Oh, damn."

"Yeah," Alex agreed. "Go to him. He's alone, and I don't know if he has anyone. He'll be admitted to the hospital soon, so hurry."

Ben nodded, swallowing hard.

"Okay, thanks," he said, before hurrying down the hall to the exam room where Zane waited.

According to the chart, he'd been beaten.

Badly.

When he pulled aside the curtain to enter Exam 2, Ben had to muffle a gasp.

Zane had been cleaned, bandaged and sutured, and he still looked a mess. His jaw was bruised and swollen, a cut had been stitched above his eye, and his lip also had a stitch where he apparently bit completely through the flesh. His arm was in an elevated sling, held immobile, until they could do a full X-ray, but Zane's chart indicated a probable break.

"Zane, honey, what happened?" Ben asked as he came into the room and approached the bedside. He laid aside the chart and grabbed the hand on Zane's uninjured side.

"I'm sorry," he said, and Ben was struck by the toneless quality to his voice. Zane sounded absolutely defeated.

Ben perched on the edge of the bed by Zane's hip. "Why are you sorry, sweetie?"

"Messed up," he whispered.

"Tell me what happened."

He almost wished Zane hadn't already had good treatment, which was completely illogical. But his hands itched to be soothing Zane, to be checking his vitals or cleaning and bandaging his injuries. To just sit here, helpless, in the face of his battery was maddening. Is this how all family members felt? No wonder some of them got so crazy.

"Step-dad," he mumbled.

"Your step-dad did this to you? Why?"

Zane answered haltingly, and Ben realized speaking was

difficult. Breathing was difficult. He added broken ribs to his mental tally of Zane's injuries.

"Dad ... didn't approve ... I'm gay," he said slowly, his voice fading in and out as he spoke. "Thought maybe my mom, but ..."

Ben leaned forward to smooth back Zane's hair. "You came out to your mom, and your step-dad assaulted you?"

Zane nodded, then winced.

"Do you have someone you want me to call?" Ben asked. At Zane's bleak expression, he had his answer. "Okay, sweetie, rest. We'll take good care of you."

He left Zane to slip down to the locker room and grab his cellphone. Screwing up his courage, he called Gage and hoped he'd answer.

Gage picked up on the first ring. "Ben?"

"Gage, you need to come down to the hospital," he said quietly. "Zane's here."

Gage followed the directions he received at admissions to the hospital room where they'd moved Zane after admitting him. He approached the doorway and paused on the threshold when he saw Ben was in the room.

Ben sat on the bed with Zane, holding his hand and leaning forward to kiss his cheek.

Gage pushed aside a flare of jealousy. He'd drawn his line in the sand, and if Ben chose to be with other men, that was at least partly his fault.

Zane needed him, so he'd man up and put his petty shit aside.

Clearing his throat, he managed a weak, "Hi, guys."

Ben straightened and turned toward him. His big brown eyes

were filled with concern. Gage wanted nothing more than to cross the room and pull him into a hug.

Then he caught sight of Zane's face.

"Jesus!" he said. "What the hell happened?"

Ben patted Zane's hand and stood up. "I should let you two talk."

As he approached the doorway, he paused next to Gage. "Don't rush him. He's probably got some broken ribs, so speaking is a little painful. Give him plenty of time to get his words out."

"Ben ..."

Ben smiled sadly. "I have to see my patients in the ER. He needs you, Gage. Just try to listen and be supportive, okay?"

Gage nodded, swallowing down the words he wanted to say.

He watched as Ben slipped out and then took his place at Zane's bedside.

"You've looked better, man. Although as tactics go, getting yourself busted up is getting you more sympathy from Ben than I ever managed."

Zane managed a pained grin. "Yeah, maybe 'cause I didn't do it to myself, klutz."

Gage forced a chuckle and grabbed a chair to pull close and sit. Resting his hands on the side of the bed, he drew on the reservoir of strength he knew Zane needed right now.

"Whatever happened, we'll make sure it doesn't happen again. I'll help you."

Tears welled up in Zane's eyes and trickled down his cheeks.

"I have nobody," he whispered, sounding absolutely wrecked.

Gage put a hand on his blanket-covered ankle. He felt like shit for not being there for Zane when he needed someone, and he wasn't going to make that mistake again. He'd find a way to deal with the pain of losing Ben without blaming Zane.

"You have me," he said. "And I'm pretty sure you have Ben."

"No!" Zane exclaimed, then groaned in pain. "Shit ... no. Ben. He's yours."

"Easy," Gage said. "I'm pretty sure Ben would argue he belongs to no man. But that's not what I meant. I meant he'd be there for you, too. Help you, if you needed."

"Oh."

"Do you need some pain medication? Have they given you anything?"

"Yeah ... wearing off."

Gage leaned forward and hit the call button, then he sat back and asked Zane to tell him everything, but to go slowly.

A nurse entered the room to administer pain meds before leaving to attend other patients.

Gage listened to Zane's story, told in bits and pieces as he was able.

Since they'd last talked in his office and he'd promised to help Zane find scholarship and grant opportunities, things had gone from bad to worse with his family. Unable to stay with friends any longer, he'd gone to his mother's place.

Zane hadn't lived with her since he was 14, he said, but he didn't know what to do. He thought she might have some advice about how to handle his father's reaction, so he came out to her, too. Zane had been less worried about her reaction, because she'd mentioned in the past she had a gay cousin and never seemed bothered by it.

He hadn't foreseen that his step-dad, Isaac, would come in during his confession, drunk as he so often was and ready to beat the gay out of Zane. His mother had gotten Isaac to stop long enough to get Zane out of the house, but she'd told him to take himself home and straighten up like his father asked.

Zane had stumbled out to the street and collapsed. He

managed to dial 911 before passing out less than 10 feet from his mother's home.

It was a heartbreaking story, and Gage realized he should have done more, even before he was angry with Zane. He should have asked Zane about other family members, about possible ports in his storm, maybe even offered him a place to stay if necessary. All the things Gage had needed as a teenager himself.

He'd taken Zane's flirtation with Ben too personally when Zane was just a kid self-destructing in the face of his father's disapproval. He'd put distance between them, even though he'd tried to be mature about it, and he'd made Zane unsure enough that he hadn't even called Gage when he ended up in ER.

Ben had done that.

"I should have never come out," Zane said miserably.

"You can't think that way, sweetie," Ben spoke up behind Gage's chair. He must have drifted in again sometime during Zane's story. At Gage's curious look, he shrugged. "I'm on a short break."

"He's right," Gage said, turning back to Zane. "You're not alone in this."

"How did your parents take it when you came out?" Zane asked tentatively, looking between them.

Ben sounded almost ashamed when he admitted his mother had been a great advocate, and his father was already gone. Zane's eyes swung to Gage, and he swallowed hard as he admitted: "Never came out. Never had anyone to tell, no family."

Ben made a sympathetic noise behind him, but he kept his eyes fixed on Zane. If it helped Zane deal, he'd share his story, unpleasant as it was.

"I know what it's like to feel abandoned by people you love, though," he said. "My mother was an addict, and child protective services took me when I was 8. She never tried to get me back, so I grew up in foster care. A little too old to draw anyone who wanted to adopt."

"Was it terrible?" Ben asked quietly.

Gage felt Ben's hand squeeze his shoulder. Normally, he'd revel in that touch, in the softness of Ben's voice. But he hated thinking about his childhood.

"They weren't all bad. I had a good foster family when I was 12, but Rebecca — my foster mom — got sick, and they couldn't keep me. I bounced to a couple more that weren't so good before they stuck me in a group home with a bunch of rebellious teens. If weren't for my high school journalism teacher, I probably would be working at McDonald's right now. But he got me invested, and he helped me get scholarships. The rest is history."

"Did you come out to him? The teacher?" Zane asked.

Gage nodded. "After I graduated. He was okay with it, but he was a pretty liberal guy."

"He wasn't ...?"

"Nope, happily married and never looked at me the wrong way. Just a good teacher."

Zane sighed. "So, a teacher came to your rescue and now you want to come to mine?"

"I'm not trying to pay it forward, Zane. I'm here because despite you being a smart-ass, we've become friends. You didn't deserve any of this, but I'll help you. If you need a place to crash, I've got a spare room. If you want someone to talk to, we're both here."

"Definitely," Ben chimed in.

"Thanks," Zane answered, somewhat uncomfortably.

Ben had to return to his work in the ER a few minutes later.

As Zane finally drifted off, Gage stayed with him, dozing in his seat, until he woke with a crick in his neck. It was nearly 3 in the morning.

Getting up, he slipped out of the room and headed down to

the ER on the off-chance Ben was still on duty. It was beyond time he tried to fix things between them, even if it meant proving his patience by actually being patient.

But by the time he got to the nurses station, Ben was already gone for the night.

14

"You should call him."

Gage tucked his phone in his back pocket and glanced over at Zane lounging on his sofa. He was still bruised, but most of the swelling had gone down in the two days he'd been there. His arm had only been fractured, so he got away with a brace and a sling instead of a full cast.

"Call who?"

Zane rolled his eyes theatrically. "Who do you think? You've only been checking for messages from Ben every five minutes."

Gage grimaced. He wished Zane was exaggerating, but he wasn't. Ben had messaged a few times to check in on Zane's condition, and Gage had soaked in each moment of contact like a flower desperately in need of sun.

Every day he was tempted to text Ben to ask him to come over. Of course, things weren't that simple. They had to get on the same page before they could move forward. And Zane was here now ... and probably would be for a while.

Gage was hoping to mediate between him and his father at some point, but Zane needed some time to heal, physically and emotionally, before braving more possible rejection. With the semester coming to an end, there shouldn't be much conflict with Zane staying in his spare room for a few weeks, though he'd keep it on the downlow to avoid the department head giving him grief.

In the meantime, Gage was hoping to get Zane's dad to attend some PFLAG meetings to meet other families of gay kids who could help him see that Zane wasn't making a choice. The man who had beaten Zane, on the other hand, would not get a second chance. Hospital policy had required that they call the police in light of Zane's injuries. His step-dad had been arrested for battery and taken a plea deal already, so at least Zane wouldn't have to testify.

"You miss him," Zane said now, bringing Gage back to his own problems. "You keep saying it's not my fault—"

"It's not, Zane!" Gage snapped. "I wish you'd stop thinking you were so enticing that Ben would leave me for a shot at you."

Gage immediately regretted his words. Pain washed over Zane's face, and the kid was already hurting enough.

"That's not what I meant," Zane said quietly, with such dignity Gage felt like even more of a shit.

He scrubbed a hand down his face. "Sorry. I'm sorry. You have enough on your plate without me snapping at you."

Zane shook his head, his eyes disbelieving.

"You're an idiot. You know that, right?"

Gage's lips quirked. "I've heard that from time to time, but why exactly am I an idiot this time?"

"Ben is crazy about you. He's not interested in me. I know that. But you guys broke up immediately after I tried to flirt with him."

"You didn't try. You did flirt, and what's more, Ben flirted back. I really don't want to talk to you about my relationship with Ben. Just please accept that you aren't the cause of our separation, okay?"

"Separation? So, this isn't permanent?"

"God, I hope not," he said fervently. "But I left the ball in Ben's court. If he wants to fix things, he'll come back to me."

"Dude, you can't do that!"

Zane immediately winced and sat back, holding his ribs, which were in fact broken but healing well.

"Easy, kid. You're still healing," Gage said.

"Listen, Gage, I know a little bit about you and Ben and how you got together."

Gage's eyebrow ticked up. "How would you know that?"

He shrugged a shoulder. "Chloe has been by a few times, and she entertained me by gossiping about your love life."

Gage groaned. "Fabulous."

"You pursued Ben from the get-go, right?"

Gage nodded, and Zane went on.

"And Ben was leery of dating because of some bad experiences, Chloe said. So, he's probably feeling like a failure when it comes to this stuff, you know? You leave the ball in his court, and he's going to think it's over."

"I told him that if or when he was ready, I'd be waiting."

"Dude, you're thinking too rationally. Think about it. Has Ben been reasonable when it comes to dating?"

Gage had to admit Zane had a point. Ben had been leery of dating, and he'd rationalized all sorts of reasons Gage would never be serious about him. Had Gage's actions just confirmed his fears? Did he view it as a break-up instead of an ultimatum, which granted, wasn't much better?

"So you're saying that even if he wants to be with me, he probably doesn't think there's a chance?"

Zane shifted, trying to get comfortable, and Gage moved to the counter to grab him some extra-strength Tylenol and a glass of water.

Gage was relieved Zane wasn't on prescribed narcotics. He

didn't feel comfortable with them in the house, and obviously the kid's pain wasn't too bad based on the pain scoring sheet they did before releasing him from the hospital.

"I don't know for sure," Zane said, accepting the pills and water with a tired smile.

He was still recovering, and when he wasn't trying to catch up on schoolwork, he was napping.

"I think you need to fight for him. Show Ben once and for all that you love him and you're not going to flake out when things get tough."

Gage returned to his chair, rubbing at his jaw as he thought it over.

Ben did have self-esteem issues, even if he denied it. He didn't believe he could hold a man's interest long-term. He preferred to hook up and run, so he didn't go through more heartbreak. Gage had promised he was different from those other men, and he was, but he hadn't given Ben enough time to trust him. He'd wanted instant trust, and he'd let his jealousy make him rash.

He'd done exactly what Ben feared: cut ties.

Gage thought a break might force Ben into realizing he wanted a serious relationship, not the half-committed dating they were doing. But thinking about it now, he could see that the problem wasn't that Ben didn't want him for a boyfriend; it was that Ben had been scared Gage would lose interest.

"Damn," he muttered.

"You see? For a kid so stupid he thinks he can lure away the hot nurse from the hot teacher, I'm not so bad."

Gage felt himself blush a little. He knew Zane found Ben attractive, but a part of him had felt a little insecure when Zane thought he could move in on his territory. That Ben would skip off with Zane.

He cleared his throat. "Okay, I think that's enough of this topic. I'm still your teacher for a couple more weeks."

Zane snorted. "I live in your house. I think the lines are a little blurry."

Gage's face must have looked a little worried because Zane seemed to read his mind.

"Dude, I just gave you a pep talk on getting Ben back. I'm not going to put the moves on you."

Gage smirked. "I didn't think you were."

"Yeah, right. One little comment about how you're hot, and you're getting all freaked out. You're my teacher. I am so not interested."

"Thanks."

"I'm not really into Ben, either," he admitted. "So, don't worry about that. Not that you need to," he hurried to say. "I'm just saying it wasn't really about that. I don't know why I did it, to be honest."

"Relax, Zane. I know. I really am telling you the truth when I say we didn't break up because of you. You might have served as a catalyst for us to confront all the things we'd been avoiding, but ... the real issue is Ben's trust. You were absolutely right before."

Zane sounded surprised. "Really?"

Gage nodded and pulled out his cellphone.

"Yes. It's time to show him how I feel, instead of just saying the words."

He excused himself and went into his bedroom for some privacy. Then he called Ben's number.

He didn't answer, but Gage reminded himself that Ben was probably at work. He texted him instead.

Let me know when you can talk

As far as messages went, it was lame. But he didn't want to

confess his feelings in a text. He wanted to call Ben, or better yet, see him.

An hour later, he got a reply.

Off at 10 tonight

Gage grinned to himself. He finally felt a sense of hope. When 10 o'clock rolled around, he was going to finally talk sense into that man.

Ben was just wrapping up his final chart updates for the night before clocking out. It had been a long day, and he was wiped out. Besides not sleeping well, he had picked up this shift on his day off because of staff shortages.

His heart tapped a nervous beat in his chest as he remembered Gage would be waiting for him.

He didn't know what Gage wanted to say, but he'd been doing a lot of thinking since their break. He'd been scared of losing Gage the night he'd flirted with Zane, desperately trying to find a way to convince himself it wasn't too late to keep it casual. But he'd been kidding himself. Gage was buried too far under his skin, and he missed him so much.

The night Zane came in battered and bruised and Gage came rushing to the hospital, Ben could hardly breathe with how much he wanted to beg Gage for another chance.

It hadn't been the right time. But maybe tonight would be.

The electronic doors of the ambulance bay slid open, followed by the chatter of paramedics as they wheeled in a gurney. Ben had been so caught up he hadn't noticed Alex take the emergency call.

One of the other nurses, Celia, and a pair of doctors were already on their way to meet the paramedics.

From this distance, he could only hear snatches of their conversation.

"Elderly woman ..."

"... acute cholecystitis ..."

He glanced toward Alex, silently asking whether he needed to stay. End of shift or not, when an emergency came in, Ben had to be prepared to lend a hand. She shook her head as she headed toward the door.

"Go home, Ben. You've been working too hard and not sleeping enough."

True enough, but maybe he'd sleep better tonight, after a heart-to-heart with Gage. Assuming the man was willing to give him another chance. Ben wouldn't blame him if he didn't want to risk it.

He stepped around the counter, intending to head to his locker to grab his belongings. But as he cast a final look toward the gurney being wheeled his direction, something about the glimpse of hand with bright gold nail polish stopped him.

He turned and paced a few steps closer, his breath catching in his chest.

"Ben? I told you to head out," Alex said impatiently. "We've got it covered."

He didn't bother responding. He stared at the woman on the gurney, fear turning his blood to ice.

"Mom?"

Tears leaked from her eyes as she whimpered in pain. Her eyes flicked to meet his, and she gasped his name.

"Ben! Bennie, it hurts."

"Oh no," Alex said, but he was oblivious. He stepped forward to grab her hand, and she clutched tight.

"What is it? Is it a heart attack? Stroke?" he asked, a little surprised at his own panicky tone ringing in his ears.

"Please step back," someone ordered, but the words barely registered under the panic ringing in his ears.

Acute cholecystitis. Ben remembered now. One of the paramedics had said it as they came in the door.

"Gallbladder attack?" he asked, but he didn't really need an answer. All of his mother's symptoms came crashing down on his head. The stomach pain. Her fear she'd had pancreatic cancer only to be told it was just a kidney infection. Yes, she'd had an infection, but it hadn't been the only problem. All along, she'd been suffering sporadic gallbladder attacks, and Ben's first guess – his first suspicion as to what might be the problem – had been right.

But he'd never followed through.

My fault. I should have taken better care of her, made sure she went back to the doctor at the first sign of trouble.

Alex grabbed his arm, tugging him back from the gurney.

He knew better than to fight; they'd just get a burly orderly to hold him back. He stared over her shoulder, desperate to keep his eyes on his mother as they wheeled her away.

"I'm here, Mom. You're in good hands, I promise," he called after her, voice shaking.

"Celia, go," Alex ordered the other nurse on duty, then turned to meet Ben's eyes. "Ben, listen to me. She's going to be okay."

"Am I right? Is it her gallbladder? Or something worse?"

She squeezed his shoulders. "You're right. They're doing emergency surgery. She's suffering a lot of abdominal pain. Paramedics asked her a lot of questions on the way here, and the symptoms add up. Her white blood cell count is elevated, so ..."

"Damn it. She went to the doctor weeks ago! She had a kidney infection and got antibiotics, but she's had too many stomachaches lately, and she's been tired. I should have realized there was more to it."

This was his fault for not going to that first appointment. What if she misunderstood? What if the doctor wanted her to return for further tests and she hadn't? It was possible the kidney infection threw the doctor off because of overlapping symptoms, but it was more likely his mother hadn't adequately explained her pain.

She got timid around doctors, and agreed with their first assessment, even if it was wrong. She didn't trust herself, and that was partly his fault. He brushed off her health concerns too often because she tended to suffer anxiety. Now she was paying for his mistake.

He might have seen that she was still suffering if he hadn't been so self-absorbed in his love affair with Gage, and after Gage left him, he'd been even more oblivious of the world around him. Instead of taking care of his mom, he'd been dodging her — afraid she'd see right through him to the heart-break underneath and ask questions he didn't want to face.

"Stop beating yourself up," Alex said. "Head up to the surgery center, okay? There's a waiting room where you'll be more comfortable. I'll check on you when I can."

Ben nodded numbly. "Okay, yeah."

"She's going to be okay. You'll see."

Gage waited in the parking lot for 15 minutes before he gave up and went inside. He would have worried that Ben ditched out on him except he'd cruised the employee parking area and spotted his car still in its spot.

He walked in the emergency room doors and approached the check-in counter. The older woman there, Sandy, recognized him. Pursing her lips, she gave him a skeptical once-over.

"What did you do to yourself this time?"

He pulled out his smile meant for charming old ladies and disgruntled helicopter parents. Nothing a college instructor loved more than a parent who still hovered over their 18-year-old. *Not.*

"I'm actually here to meet one of the nurses."

Her eyebrow ticked up. She didn't look impressed by the smile. "If they're here, they're working."

"I know, but Ben is actually supposed to be off shift by now."

"Ben, you say?" Her demeanor seemed to change. "Well, now, I can't tell you why he hasn't come out. I'm sure there's a good reason."

She lifted a receiver and held it out to him. "I'm connecting you to the nurses station. You can ask there."

He just had time to mumble a quick thank-you before a crisp, no-nonsense voice was answering. "This is the Ashe ER."

"Hi, I'm looking for Ben Griggs."

"Who is this?"

"It's Gage—"

"Oh, thank God." The voice on the line changed. The owner was no longer an all business operator, but a real live human who expressed emotion. "Where are you right now?"

"I'm in the ER waiting room."

"That's great," she said in relief. "Listen, I don't know care what you two are fighting about—"

"Is this Alex?" he asked.

She talked over him, not bothering to answer, but he recognized the tone of her voice now.

"—but he's up there all alone, and he needs someone right now. So, you're going to be that someone. You can be another in a line of dickheads who don't appreciate Ben later. But right now, you'll put his needs first."

"Alex!" he barked when she paused to take a breath. Gage feared the lecture was nowhere near an end, and he needed information, not misguided scolding. "Where is he? What happened?"

"His mother came in tonight, and not as a visitor. He's up in the surgery center alone because I can't leave here."

Oh shit, not his mom.

"I was nearly desperate enough to call Dr. Johnston and see if he could sit with him," Alex continued.

The asshole doctor who stared at Ben's ass? No fucking way.

"Don't you dare," Gage spat, before taking a breath and pushing down his anger. Alex obviously didn't know the full story about them, and he didn't have time to give it to her.

"I can't hash this out right now, Alex, but I can promise you I will be there for him. Now and any other time he needs me."

He heard her sigh of relief. "That's great, Gage. I really liked you two together."

"I have to get up there."

"Yes, you do. Take the elevators right off the vending area to the second floor. Turn right, and there's a waiting room at the end of the hall. Go now."

There was a click in his ear, followed by the dial tone. He handed the receiver back to Sandy, and she did a remarkable impersonation of someone who hadn't eavesdropped on an entire conversation.

He gestured over his shoulder. "Thanks, I have to run."

She waved a hand. "Go on, sweetie. Don't keep him waiting."

He turned and jogged for the elevator, his heart beating fast. He knew there'd be nothing to do but wait and worry once he got up there, but the thought of Ben losing his mother scared the crap out of him. He didn't know how Ben would handle that, or how he'd cope with seeing Ben in so much pain, but he resolved to be there for him either way.

He wasn't walking away again, no matter how hard Ben pushed him.

15

Ben looked up at the sound of approaching feet, anxious for news of his mother. She wasn't young, and the one update he'd gotten didn't reassure him. The surgeon had warned him that although it was a relatively routine surgery, things were always less certain with older patients. There was a chance of complications with anyone, and the odds went up with the patient's age.

Ben knew that already, of course, but hearing it again added about a pound of anxiety in his chest that made it hard to breathe.

He blinked his eyes, confused by the sight of a ragged Gage. There were shadows under his eyes, and his skin was too pale. He looked like he hadn't slept in a week.

"Did you get hurt again?" he demanded.

"Yeah," Gage admitted.

"What happened?" he asked, rising to his feet to look Gage over more carefully. "What did you do this time?"

To his surprise, Gage drew him in for a tight hug.

"Doesn't matter. I did it to myself," he said gruffly. Pulling back, he met Ben's eyes. "Your mom is in surgery?"

Ben slumped, the exhaustion and stress of moments before returning forcefully now that he was no longer distracted by Gage's surprise appearance.

"Yeah." He sank back into his seat wearily. "Who told you?"

"Alex. I called her when you didn't meet me at the end of your shift."

Oh, crap. He'd completely forgotten about agreeing to meet Gage at the end of his shift. It'd been on his mind all night, until he'd seen his mother on that gurney. Then all thoughts had been shoved out of his head by worry and fear.

Of course, Gage wouldn't come up here if he was injured. That didn't make any sense. It was possible Ben was just a bit delirious from lack of sleep. He hadn't had a decent night's rest since losing Gage.

He looked again at Gage, relieved that he was okay, other than tired and stressed. Maybe he wasn't sleeping so well, either.

"Sorry I didn't call," Ben said.

Gage took the plastic seat next to his and put an arm around his shoulders, encouraging Ben to lean into his body. Ben was too tired to fight it. He didn't want to fight it.

"So, tell me about what's going on with your mom," Gage said quietly.

"Supposed to be a routine gallbladder removal," he mumbled.

"But it's not?"

"She arrived by ambulance, in severe pain, so you know ... it's not a scheduled operation. Plus, her age is a concern, and I'm a little rattled because I should have seen it coming. I did, but then she went to the doctor and was diagnosed with a kidney infection. She still had pain after that, and I was too caught up in my own life to make sure she was okay."

"Shhh." Gage rubbed circles on his back, his touch a

soothing counterpoint to Ben's worried tension. "She'd still have to have the surgery, right?"

"Yes. There's no other option, really."

"Okay then, stop beating yourself up. She's getting treatment now."

Ben nodded, taking a deep breath. Gage was right. What-ifs weren't going to help anything now, but he hated that she'd gone to emergency surgery in so much pain instead of a nice, planned procedure where they could both emotionally prepare themselves.

"How long does the surgery take?"

"About two hours," Ben said. "Maybe a little longer, but that's the average."

"Okay, so we'll wait together."

Ben tilted his head to look up at Gage's face. He hadn't forgotten, even in these circumstances, that this man had walked away from him. That he'd screwed up the best thing to ever happen to him.

"Why are you here?" he asked.

He'd been wondering all night what Gage might want to talk about. Maybe he wanted to fix things between them. Then again, maybe something new happened with Zane, or Gage just wanted closure between them. They'd left things unresolved, not together but not fully broken up, though it sure as hell felt like he'd been dumped. His heart ached for Gage on a daily basis.

Ben had hardly dared to hope for the outcome he wanted: one more chance with Gage, one more chance to give him the trust he deserved.

"For you," Gage said quietly. "Because I love you, and I can't just walk away, despite what I said. I'll wait for you to trust me. You don't have to prove anything. But I promise, from now on, *I'll* trust *you*. If that's even what you want."

"Gage ..."

His voice broke, and he had to clear his throat. Before he could say anything more, Gage pressed a finger to his lips, silencing him.

"Don't say anything right now," he said. "Don't worry about anything. You need me, so I'm here. If you want me to leave later, I will. But just let me be here with you for now."

Ben bit his lip. He was never going to send Gage away. He had been on the verge of telling Gage he loved him, too. But his mind was divided between Gage and his mother, and Gage was right that now wasn't the time for them to talk.

"Thank you," he said. "How's Zane?"

"He's doing better physically. We have some work to do emotionally. I talked to his biological father about attending some informational PFLAG meetings. There's not much hope for mending fences with that asshole of a step-dad, or even his mother. But I'm hoping to work toward some kind of relationship between him and his dad. But right now, Zane needs time."

Ben took hold of Gage's hand and squeezed his fingers. The touch of him, skin to skin, was such a relief Ben had to close his eyes a moment and push down the emotions that wanted to bubble out.

"He's so lucky to have a teacher like you, Gage."

"He's a good kid," Gage said, but he turned the conversation back to Ben. He knew Ben had a tendency to take care of everyone around him, but Gage was here to support him, and he wasn't going to let anyone – even Ben – stop him. "Have you eaten? I could get you something."

Ben shook his head. "Not hungry. God, I just need her to be okay."

"You and your mom are close, huh?"

Ben felt a smile tug at his lips. "The closest. She's my best friend and my mom all rolled into one."

"That's great. Based on what you told Zane, I take it she was always supportive about you being gay?"

Ben snorted with amusement. "If you can call trying to constantly set me up with every gay relative of a friend of a friend supportive, then yeah. She was a little surprised when I came out, but she's always been good at rolling with whatever life brings."

"Well, there you go," Gage said. "She's good at rolling with it. She'll roll with this too."

Gage kissed his cheek, and pulled him closer, encouraging him to lay his head on his shoulder once more.

"Just close your eyes and relax for a minute. I'll let you know if anyone comes out to update you."

"Okay," he mumbled. "You look like crap. Are you okay?"

He felt Gage's body vibrate with a chuckle. "Thanks. It's been a rough couple of weeks, but I feel a lot better now."

Ben sighed. "Me too."

Gage shifted carefully in his seat, trying to ease his numb ass and stiff shoulder without jostling Ben. He was awake, but he'd fallen into a dazed trance that told Gage he was only half present. He would probably be out cold if it weren't for the gnawing worry about his mom.

They'd been waiting about three hours now. Ben had lost his cool after the two-hour mark came and went without an update. Gage had talked him off the edge of hysteria more than once. He'd asked Ben all kinds of medical questions, which seemed to engage the nurse side of him. He'd calmed down and talked through all the reasons a surgery might run long, explaining everything to Gage as if he were the worried family member.

It wasn't entirely reassuring. There was a list of possible complications, from reactions to the anesthesia to nicking an organ that needed repair or discovery of another problem that required an emergency fix. But it seemed to calm Ben down all the same, so Gage tucked away that little trick for future reference, while hoping he'd never need it.

A door opened, and a woman in blue scrubs stepped through. Her eyes were fixed in their direction.

Before he could alert Ben, the man had jumped to his feet. He rushed forward to meet the surgeon.

"What happened in there? It's been three hours!"

Gage got to his feet and approached. The surgeon looked calm and collected despite Ben's emotional outburst.

"We removed her gallbladder, it was necrotic and full of stones."

"Okay, I expected that. But why did it take so long?"

"She's fine," she repeated firmly. "We had to wait for an OR to open up, so we did a sonogram before surgery to be certain of the diagnosis."

"But she was in so much pain," Ben protested.

"At her age, even routine surgery is not a decision to be taken lightly. We needed to rule out other possibilities. As it turns out, we were able to perform a laparoscopic removal, so her recovery time should be minimal. A few days and she'll be on her feet and just fine."

It was good news, but Ben swayed on his feet.

"Thank God," he said faintly.

Gage wrapped an arm around his waist, hauling him in against his side.

"I knew it was just routine," Ben told the doctor, his voice still weak. "But you just think about everything that could go wrong. Especially at her age."

The surgeon smiled in understanding, and reached out to squeeze his hand.

"She's still waking up from the anesthesia, but a nurse will be out to take you back to her room once she's transferred from recovery."

"Thank you," he said.

After the doctor left, Ben sagged against Gage in relief. But there was something in his worried brown eyes that set off alarm bells. He chewed on his lip, as he always did when troubled.

"Why are you so worried?" Gage asked. "It sounded like good news. Did I miss something?"

Ben shook his head. "No, it's very good news. She's going to be okay. But ..."

"What?"

"I think I should move her in with me."

Gage didn't follow his logic. "I thought the surgeon said she'd recover in a few days."

"Yeah, this time. But what if she has a heart attack next time? Or a stroke? What if she can't get to a phone?"

"You can't be with her every minute."

Ben nodded. "I know, but ... she doesn't have my father. She's all alone, and she's not young anymore. I already let her down once, with this gallbladder thing. If we'd been living together, I wouldn't have missed it."

Gage didn't know what to say to that. He squeezed Ben against his side, trying to offer silent comfort.

Ben stared across the room, then shook his head.

"I'm sorry, Gage," he said at last.

"Sorry?"

He looked up at him, and his expression gutted Gage. Those brown eyes rivaled the biggest, saddest pair of puppy dog eyes he'd ever seen.

"I really wanted to fix things with you, but now ..."

Gage's heart flipped in his chest. "So, let's fix things."

"How can I ask you to take this on? You want to make a life with a man, not a man and his mother. She's going to need me, and I have to put her first."

Gage drew Ben into his arms and held him for a long moment. He understood where Ben was coming from, but he couldn't help wondering if this was just another way to run from him.

"We can make this work."

Ben drew back, eyes wide. "We can?"

"Did I imagine that my future boyfriend would need to live with his mom? No. But then I didn't think I'd be moving one of my students in with me either. Do what you need to do. You're still the man I love."

Ben's face crumpled, and he buried his face in Gage's neck.

"You're sure?" he whispered.

"Yes."

"What about the future, though? Don't you want to live with me at some point? Get married? Not that I'm suggesting we do it right away. But ... eventually ... maybe?"

Gage smiled to see the red staining Ben's cheeks.

"We can still do all that. It'll just look different than we imagined."

Ben hugged him so tight he could hardly breathe. "You really are a daring man."

Gage laughed breathlessly. "So, can you finally admit there are redeeming qualities to adrenaline junkies?"

Ben pulled back to meet his eyes. "Guess I'm more exciting than I thought."

"You got that right," Gage said, kissing his cheek and whispering in his ear. "You always make my heart beat faster."

Then Ben said the words Gage needed to hear, the words that ensured he'd never walk away again no matter what happened. He'd happily live with all of Ben's relatives – a mother, a distant aunt or cousin – so long as he got to keep the man in his arms.

"I love you."

EPILOGUE

Six months later …

"Hurry," Ben gasped, "my mom—"

"I know."

Gage covered his mouth with his own, swallowing the rest of his words as he pumped deep inside Ben. Their sweat-slicked bodies slid together feverishly, both of them well aware they were short on time.

Ben panted against Gage's mouth as the man hit his prostate again and again. He reached for his cock, but Gage swatted his arm away and took him in his larger hand. He stroked roughly, matching the strokes of his hand to the rhythm of his thrusts, and Ben came apart.

Shuddering, he spilled between them, and a few thrusts later, Gage followed.

He collapsed beside Ben, breathing hard. When he caught his breath, he nudged Ben.

"You take the first shower, so you have time to fix your hair."

Ben jabbed him in the ribs with an elbow. "Shut up!"

Gage laughed and kissed him on the cheek. "I love your hair, hon. It's obviously the only reason I ever wanted to date you."

Ben glared playfully and rolled out of bed.

"Fine, but you have to wrap the present! " he called as he dashed into the bathroom for a super fast shower. His mother's birthday party was starting in 20 minutes, and they were almost certain to be late.

Gage had delighted in teasing Ben about his grooming habits since they'd moved in together and he'd discovered that Ben's hair didn't naturally fall in perfect waves and his skin wasn't so clear and smooth because he didn't take care of it.

Yes, Ben had a skin care routine and he styled his hair. It was really his only vanity, so he didn't feel bad about it. Plus, Gage *did* love the way he looked. Ben still liked to remind Gage of the nickname he'd given him before they properly knew each other.

Nurse Hotness.

This Nurse Hotness didn't intend to become Nurse Boring just because he and Gage lived together now. Or would soon be getting engaged, if he had anything to say about it.

After getting clean, he opened the door and told Gage he could shower while Ben engaged in his time-consuming grooming.

Gage was in and out before he'd finished styling his hair. A few minutes later, Gage called him in an exasperated voice.

"We're going to be late!"

"Like she'll be surprised," he said with a grin as he joined Gage in the living room, where he waited with a small package wrapped in silver and blue.

Luckily, his mom's place was only a five-minute drive away.

Despite Ben's fears after his mom's surgery and his determination that she'd need to move in with him, he hadn't accounted for his mom's reaction. She'd flat-out refused to live with him, and when he'd become so worried he broke down in front of her, she'd agreed to move into a retirement community with safety measures in place.

She'd been so happy for him, and she hadn't wanted to endanger his fragile new relationship. That only made him love her more.

Thankfully, six months later she was still vibrant and healthy, and she'd made a lot of friends in her new home. In fact, Ben knew her party would be large and boisterous with old ladies who wouldn't hesitate to pinch his cheeks and tell him how adorable he was.

"Think she'll like the present?" Gage asked.

"You got her a charm bracelet with unicorns and mermaids," Ben said. "She'll love it."

Gage dropped a kiss on Ben's temple. "Good, let's go."

"Wait," Ben said, grabbing his hand before he could walk out the door.

"Thank you."

"For picking out her gift? That was nothing. I love her—"

"No, I know," Ben said. "I just ... I know how you feel about birthdays."

"That really only applies to my own."

"Yeah, well I'm working on that," Ben said with a teasing smile. "But what I'm trying to say is that I feel really lucky to have you."

"I feel the same," Gage said simply, and leaned down to kiss Ben.

Their lips met is a soft slide, and when Ben pulled back, he touched Gage's face gently. His heart was full of affection for the man, and he thanked all that was holy that Gage had been a patient, tenacious man who hadn't given up on him.

"I know I didn't make it easy for you to love me, so thank you."

"Well, you're incredibly easy now," Gage teased, grabbing

Ben's ass and squeezing until he squeaked and swatted his arm with his free hand. "So, thank you."

"Smart-ass," Ben muttered, before stepping out the door. "We better get over there before you have to explain to my mother you were too busy feeling up her son to be on time."

"She'll just invite me to use the bedroom," Gage said with a grin.

Ben laughed and rolled his eyes. "God, she probably would."

Gage unlocked the car doors, and they slid in. Just as he turned the ignition, Ben grabbed his arm.

"Oh shoot, I forgot to feed the cat!"

He moved toward the door, but Gage stopped him.

"I'll do it. He loves me best," he teased, and Ben laughed as he watched his boyfriend trot back to the front door.

Ironically, it was true. Bruiser had warmed up to Gage, just as Ben had, and they both adored the man who'd snuck into their lives despite their hackles being raised.

Apparently, Gage had the special touch. Whether feline or man, he knew how to make them purr with contentment.

— fin —

THANK YOU FOR READING!

Thank you for reading *Heart Trouble*. I hope you enjoyed this sweet m/m romance story. If you would be so kind as to leave a review, it would be appreciated! You can get bonus content and giveaway opportunities through my mailing list! Sign up at
http://www.tinyurl.com/djandcompany.

I also encourage you to join my FB group DJ and Company for fun teasers and other extras.

You can connect with me on social media in other ways, as well!

facebook.com/AuthorDJJamison

twitter.com/DJ_Jamison_

goodreads.com/DJ_Jamison

bookbub.com/authors/dj-jamison

ABOUT THE AUTHOR

DJ Jamison grew up in the Midwest, where she was the living embodiment of the phrase "red-headed stepchild." Growing up in a working class family, DJ was determined to create a more secure future by graduating from college and was the first in her immediate family to do so. As a bookworm, though, DJ secretly always wanted to be an author. She went on to work in the newspaper industry for more than a decade, which came in handy when she began a series centered on a small-town news staff and their love connections. When she's not laboring over her works of fiction, she reads copious amounts of books on her phone. She's married with two sons, two fish, one snake, and a sadistic cat named Birdie.

BOOKS BY DJ JAMISON

Standalone books

Love by Number

Yours for the Holiday

The Espinoza Boys

Earning Edie (m/f)

Catching Jaime (m/m)

Made in the USA
Middletown, DE
18 December 2020

29051756R00108